Melissa Kenneay knew how to make a man ache.

To make a man want. And Rob didn't want to do either of those things.

He stubbornly continued to wash the dishes, reluctant to acknowledge that he was alone with Melissa.

But she didn't sit down at the kitchen table. Instead, he suddenly found her beside him, a towel in her hands.

His head whipped around to stare at the beautiful woman beside him. Tonight her dress was mint-green, almost the color of her eyes. It fit snugly from the waist up, and he suddenly dropped the dish he had been washing. Fortunately, the water cushioned its landing and it didn't break. It only splashed him with water.

Melissa took the towel and began blotting his shirt and chest.

He thought he'd die.

The Circle K Sisters

Dear Reader,

Looking for sensational summer reads? All year we've been celebrating Silhouette's 20th Anniversary with special titles, and this month's selections are just the warm, romantic tales you've been seeking!

Bestselling author Stella Bagwell continues the newest Romance promotion, AN OLDER MAN. *Falling for Grace* hadn't been his intention, particularly when his younger, *pregnant* neighbor was carrying his nephew's baby! Judy Christenberry's THE CIRCLE K SISTERS miniseries comes back to Romance this month, when sister Melissa enlists the temporary services of *The Borrowed Groom*. Moyra Tarling's *Denim & Diamond* pairs a rough-hewn single dad with the expectant woman he'd once desired beyond reason...but let get away.

Valerie Parv unveils her romantic royalty series THE CARRAMER CROWN. When a woman literally washes ashore at the feet of the prince, she becomes companion to *The Monarch's Son*...but will she ever become the monarch's wife? Julianna Morris's BRIDAL FEVER! persists when *Jodie's Mail-Order Man* discovers her heart's desire: the *brother* of her mail-order groom! And Martha Shields's *Lassoed!* is the perfect Opposites Attract story this summer. The sparks between a rough-and-tumble rodeo champ and the refined beauty sent to photograph him jump off every page!

In future months, look for STORKVILLE, USA, our newest continuity series. And don't miss the charming miniseries THE CHANDLERS REQUEST... from *New York Times* bestselling author Kasey Michaels.

Happy reading!

Mary-Theresa Hussey

Mary-Theresa Hussey
Senior Editor

Please address questions and book requests to:
Silhouette Reader Service
U.S.: 3010 Walden Ave., P.O. Box 1325, Buffalo, NY 14269
Canadian: P.O. Box 609, Fort Erie, Ont. L2A 5X3

The Borrowed Groom

JUDY CHRISTENBERRY

Silhouette

ROMANCE™

Published by Silhouette Books

America's Publisher of Contemporary Romance

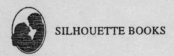

SILHOUETTE BOOKS

ISBN 0-373-19457-9

THE BORROWED GROOM

This edition published by arrangement with Harlequin Books S.A.

® and TM are trademarks of Harlequin Books S.A., used under license. Trademarks indicated with ® are registered in the United States Patent and Trademark Office, the Canadian Trade Marks Office and in other countries.

Visit Silhouette at www.eHarlequin.com

Printed in U.S.A.

Books by Judy Christenberry

Silhouette Romance

The Nine-Month Bride #1324
*Marry Me, Kate #1343
*Baby in Her Arms #1350
*A Ring for Cinderella #1356
†Never Let You Go #1453
†The Borrowed Groom #1457

*Lucky Charm Sisters
†The Circle K Sisters

JUDY CHRISTENBERRY

has been writing romances for fifteen years because she loves happy endings as much as her readers do. She's a bestselling writer for Harlequin American Romance, but she has a long love of traditional romances and is delighted to tell a story that brings those elements to the reader. A former French teacher, Judy now devotes her time to writing. She hopes readers have as much fun reading her stories as she does writing them. She spends her spare time reading, watching her favorite sports teams and keeping track of her two daughters. Judy's a native Texan, who recently moved to Tempe, Arizona.

IT'S OUR 20th ANNIVERSARY!
We'll be celebrating all year,
Continuing with these fabulous titles,
On sale in July 2000.

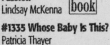

Chapter One

"Terri!"

The roar of a frustrated man's voice penetrated the warm happiness of Melissa Kennedy's kitchen, bringing alarm to her guest's face.

The young girl gasped and leaped to her feet. "That's my dad!" She seemed prepared to race out of the house.

"I'll invite him in," Melissa said, motioning with her hand for Terri Hanson to sit back down. She didn't like the look of apprehension on the child's face. If this man abused his daughter, he'd have her to deal with.

After all, her dream, one she'd been able to realize when her aunt Beulah had died and left her and her sisters a fortune, was to protect children. She'd built her new home here on the family ranch, a few yards from the original homestead, so she'd have room for the foster children she hoped to care for.

"Mr. Hanson?" she called, after stepping out onto the porch, staring at the man standing in front of the nearby manager's house, his hands cocked on his hips, his hat pulled low. "Terri's here with me."

At first she thought he wasn't going to move. Then he covered the ground between them quickly. Though he was a handsome man, broad-shouldered, narrow-hipped, he wasn't happy. The urge to back up a step or two struck her, but she held her ground.

He stopped at the bottom of the steps and touched his hat with his fingers. "Ma'am. Would you please ask Terri to come here?" His face was stern, unyielding, his gaze cold.

"I have a better idea. Why don't you join us? I'm Melissa, Abby's sister. Terri is having a snack with us. I think there are a few cookies left over." She gave him her best smile. Abby, her older sister, had told her that she had hired Rob Hanson to manage the cattle operations of the family ranch.

"No, ma'am. My daughter, please."

As if she were holding Terri hostage!

"I'll be glad to call your daughter, Mr. Hanson, but I wanted to discuss a…a proposition with you." One that had struck her when she saw how well Terri dealt with the two young foster children who had arrived last night. "It will be more comfortable if we hold our discussion inside."

He stood there frowning at her, and she considered that he might stay that way until Terri appeared. She tried again. "I'm sorry I didn't meet you and Terri yesterday, but I had business to take care of. Please let me extend a welcome to you now."

"Thanks. What proposition?"

A man of few words.

"I think we should discuss it inside." She could be as stubborn as the cowboy. Turning her back to him, she walked into the house, leaving the door open.

Damn! Just what he didn't need. A woman. A soft, feminine woman, wanting something.

The last time he'd given in to a woman's softness, let her have her way, he'd been left with a three-month-old baby to raise. He'd vowed then and there to keep his distance.

But Rob Hanson liked his new job. Abby Kennedy seemed a fair woman, a woman who thought like a man. He needed a place to settle down for a while, give Terri some stability after uprooting her. He didn't want to leave.

So he'd best make amends with the boss's sister.

He strode up the steps, across the porch and into the house, removing his Stetson as he did so. He was immediately struck by the homeyness of the place. The kind of home a man dreams about. Cool, quiet, inviting.

This was worse than he'd thought it would be.

"In here, Mr. Hanson," that warm voice called, luring him deeper and deeper into the trap.

The kitchen was large, bright, filled with mouth-watering scents…and three girls. He stared at his daughter, his gaze conveying his displeasure.

"Hi, Dad. Melissa invited me to have cookies and milk with her and the girls, and I didn't think you'd mind." Terri spoke quickly, obviously hoping to get

her excuses in before he ordered her back to their
new house.

"I told her I thought it would be all right since
I'm Abby's sister," his hostess added.

A lot of things sprang to mind to tell the woman,
but he decided it would be safest to ignore her. If he
could. She was mighty distracting. "I was worried
about you," he said to his daughter. The emotion,
the panic he'd experienced when he found his daughter missing, burred his voice.

Terri slipped from her chair and ran to slide her
arms around his waist and give him a hug. She
thought she was getting too old for hugs these days,
but he wasn't. He still needed to hold her close.

"Sorry, Dad," she whispered.

"I know, baby. It's all right," he whispered in
return.

Over Terri's shoulder, the two little girls stared at
him, scared looks on their faces.

"I didn't mean to growl so," he said both to them
and his hostess.

Terri pulled away. "This is my dad," she said.

He loved the pride in her voice. He wasn't sure he
deserved it, but it kept him standing a little straighter.

"Let me introduce Jessica and Mary Ann," Melissa Kennedy said, moving to stand beside the two
girls. "They're staying with me."

Rob said his hellos, adding a smile to convince
them he wasn't a bad guy. He didn't succeed.

"Terri, would you mind taking the girls upstairs
and helping them wash up? I think they have chocolate all over their faces."

"We didn't mean to!" one of them protested.

Rob turned sharp eyes on his hostess. Was she one of those neat freaks, not wanting a thing out of place?

Melissa bent over and kissed first one child's cheek and then the other little girl's. "Of course you didn't. I made messy cookies. And it won't take a minute to clean up." Even as she smiled at the girls, she looked at Terri, a question in her gaze.

"Sure. It's okay, isn't it, Dad? It won't take long."

"Okay."

The children went eagerly with Terri. He didn't know if it was his daughter's charm or fear of him that motivated them, but they were quickly out of the room.

Melissa gestured to one of the chairs at the table. Reluctantly, he moved to it and stood waiting for her to join him.

She placed a new plate of cookies on the table. "Did you want milk with the cookies? Or I have soda or coffee."

"Milk will be fine."

He wondered if he could resist the cookies. Home-baked cookies were rare in his life. But they were part of the trap. The scent of fresh cookies laced with chocolate drifted up to him and he knew resistance wasn't going to happen.

Melissa set a glass of milk in front of him, then pulled out the chair next to him and sat down.

After he lowered himself onto the chair next to her, she nudged the plate closer to the empty saucer she'd given him. "Help yourself."

Maybe if he only ate one it wouldn't be so bad.

She leaned toward him and he discovered something more tempting than warm, homemade cookies.

Green eyes, laced with dark lashes, faced him. Beneath them was a soft, kissable mouth, faintly pink. Smooth skin, framed by a halo of dark curls, added to the picture.

He stopped, with the cookie halfway to his mouth. Putting it back down, he said carefully, "What is it you wanted to talk to me about?" He had to get out of there—quick.

"I wanted to offer Terri a job."

He stood, reaching for his hat where he'd hung it on the chair. "My daughter doesn't need to work." He kept his voice polite but firm. Then he made his escape.

He'd almost made it out of the kitchen, ready to shout for Terri, when Melissa caught hold of his arm.

"Mr. Hanson, let me explain."

"There's nothing to explain. I don't know what she told you, but Terri's only twelve." He glared at her.

"I know that. But I need help with the kids, and I thought she might be bored this summer, since she's new to the area."

She needed help with two little kids? Yeah, right. She expected someone else to do the work while she sat around watching television, he guessed. He hated those kinds of women. "Sorry. You find someone else to be your slave. It won't be my daughter."

She seemed taken aback by his vehemence. Good. He didn't want anyone taking Terri's childhood away from her.

"You don't understand. It wouldn't be all day. I could hire her for three or four hours a day."

"Hire me?" Terri said, tumbling down the stairs

in excitement, clearly having overheard the woman. "You want to offer me a job?"

Rob silently groaned. He knew what was coming. "Now, Terri, it's time for us to get out of Ms. Kennedy's way. Let's go."

"But, Dad—"

"Mr. Hanson!"

"Thank you, ma'am, for your kindness. Terri." He spoke his daughter's name with all the authority he possessed. He knew she wouldn't want to go. Already she'd been taken in by the woman's trap.

But not him.

Hell! He hadn't even tasted one of those cookies.

"Yes, Dad," Terri said, her chin dropping.

He hated to disappoint her. But it was for her own good. He slapped his Stetson onto his head, took hold of Terri's hand, and led her out of that den of motherhood designed to capture the unwary.

Melissa spent the entire afternoon thinking about Rob Hanson and his daughter.

If she hadn't seen the way he'd softened, the way he'd wrapped his arms around Terri when she'd hugged him, Melissa might think the man was an ogre.

But she'd seen the love in his eyes.

So, he hadn't understood her offer. Somehow he suspected her of wanting to take advantage of Terri. Instead she'd had the girl's best interest at heart.

Well, she'd benefit from Terri's working for her, of course. But a twelve-year-old girl, stuck on her own all summer, not knowing anyone, would be bored to tears. And lonesome.

She wanted to help Terri if she could. But most of all, she wanted to fulfill her dream. When their aunt Beulah had taken her and her two sisters in after they were orphaned as children, she'd saved them from what they considered a fate worse than death.

Social Services had intended to split the sisters up, placing them in three foster homes. After the tragedy of their parents' deaths, they hadn't thought they could bear losing each other, too.

After sixteen years together on the ranch, where Aunt Beulah had taught them about life, she'd died last summer. And they'd been shocked to discover Aunt Beulah had had a lot of money, invested when the oil boom had struck Oklahoma.

The three sisters, her, Abby and Beth, the youngest, had decided to keep the ranch, but each sister would be free to follow her dream. Beth had thought she wanted to be a barrel racer, following the rodeo circuit.

Melissa smiled. That dream had been exchanged for Jed Davis. He'd been Beth's instructor in barrel racing. Now they were man and wife, living across the road, on Ellen Wisner's old farm. Ellen had come to work for the Kennedy sisters as housekeeper. After buying it from her, Jed was turning it into a highly respected training center for rodeo horses and riders.

Abby seemed content running the ranch. She worked hard, riding all day and studying books on ranching into the night. Melissa worried that she might not be happy, but Abby had the right to make her own choices.

Melissa had always been more interested in home-making than ranching. She loved to cook, to clean, to decorate. She had known immediately what she wanted to do with her share of the inheritance. After finding Ellen to replace her at the homestead, she'd set about building her dream house near Aunt Beulah's home.

Then she'd gone to Social Services to apply as a foster parent. She wanted to take in siblings, like her and her sisters, who otherwise might be separated. She wanted to do for other children what Aunt Beulah had done for them.

Charles Graham, the local head of Social Services, however, didn't like the idea of a single woman taking in children. Though he couldn't legally refuse her, she knew she'd have to struggle with his prejudices.

When Jessica and Mary Ann Whitney had been abandoned, he'd had no option but to give them to Melissa because he had no other openings. So her dream was coming true.

With Terri's help, the two little girls would relax, feel more at home. And if she was successful with these two children, maybe Mr. Graham would have more faith in Melissa's abilities. She was having to play it by ear with the children because they didn't have any background information. They'd been abandoned by people who were apparently passing through town.

It hadn't taken Melissa long to figure out the little girls had been mistreated. Their fear of punishment if they made any noise or caused any trouble made her want to cry.

Only when Terri had joined them had the two little girls smiled and relaxed a little.

After dinner, she bathed the little girls, who seemed surprised that they would take another bath so soon after last night's, and tucked them into bed. After reading them a story, she had them repeat the simple prayer she'd learned as a child. Then she tucked the cover under their chins.

"Do you remember meeting Ellen today?" she asked, naming the housekeeper at Abby's house.

They nodded, their eyes big.

"She's going to come stay with you for a few minutes while I go talk to Terri's daddy, to see if she can come play with us again."

The girls' eyes grew even bigger. Jessica raised up on one elbow and whispered, "He's big."

Melissa blinked. "Well, yes, he is, but—"

"He might hurt you."

She took in a deep breath. "Did your daddy hurt you?"

Mary Ann scooted closer to her sister. Jessica stared at her. Finally she whispered, "He said we were bad."

"Oh, darling," Melissa whispered, leaning over to hug both girls. "Your daddy was wrong. And Mr. Hanson isn't going to hurt me. You want Terri to come play, don't you?"

Both girls nodded.

"Then don't worry about me. Ellen will be here if you need anything, and I'll come see you when I get back." She figured they'd be asleep, but she hoped her promise would keep them from worrying.

She returned to the kitchen to retrieve the plate of cookies she'd offered Rob Hanson earlier. He'd seemed interested, but her question about Terri had put him off.

"Melissa? May I come in?"

Melissa hurried to let Ellen in. "Thanks for coming, Ellen. The girls are still a little nervous about being here."

"No problem. Are they in bed?"

"Yes. I promise I won't be long."

Darkness came late to Texas in summer. It was almost nine o'clock and the sun had gone, but a soft evening glow had settled over the land. It was Melissa's favorite time of the day.

She rapped softly on the door of the manager's house. It hadn't been used in a while, and she wondered how the man and his daughter had settled in. If she hadn't had the girls arrive, she would've offered to help clean it up, but she suspected Ellen had helped out.

The door swung open and Rob Hanson stared at her.

"Mr. Hanson, I wondered if I might talk to you."

He wanted to send her on her way. She could read that message on his handsome face.

He said quietly, "Terri's already asleep."

"Good. We could talk out here, on the porch." She waited patiently for him to respond, but she worried that he might reject her overture.

With an abrupt nod, he stepped out and closed the door behind him. Using a gentlemanly gesture, he waved toward the steps.

As she sat down, she held the plate, covered with foil, on her lap. She'd said nothing about her peace offering, but she noted his gaze on it.

"You didn't get a chance to have a cookie today. I brought some for you to eat later."

He frowned at her. "Lady, I can't be bought with cookies."

She arched one eyebrow. "I never thought you could, Mr. Hanson." Even frowning, the man was handsome. Did he realize it? She figured he did. Most men knew when they appealed to women.

"What do you want?" he asked abruptly, shifting away from her on the step.

"I wanted to explain my job offer to Terri."

"We're not interested." He stared straight ahead of him, refusing to look at her.

"I think you didn't understand my reasons for wanting to hire Terri. She's—"

"You don't want to look after your own kids. That's why you wanted to hire her, and I don't approve."

Melissa was slow to anger. She'd always been the peacemaker in her family. But this man was beginning to grate on her. She was tired of being accused of something. She wasn't sure what.

"Mr. Hanson, first of all, those are not my children."

He slewed around to stare at her. "Then why are they living with you?"

"I'm their foster mother."

"I thought you were single. Miss Abby said—"

"What has that got to do with anything?"

"Foster mothers usually have foster fathers."

She felt her cheeks heating up but she refused to look away from his hard stare. "Most of them do. I don't."

"Why did you volunteer if you don't want to do the work?"

She slowly counted to ten, keeping her breathing even. "Mr. Hanson, I have no problem with the work. But Jessica and Mary Ann relaxed for the first time today when Terri joined us. I thought if she came over every day and played with them, they would feel more comfortable. And I thought Terri might enjoy it, too." She crossed her arms over her chest and waited for the man's apology.

Rob wished she wouldn't cross her arms like that. It brought attention to a certain part of her anatomy he'd rather ignore.

"Well?" she finally prompted.

"Well, what?" He'd gotten distracted and wasn't sure what she expected him to say.

"Aren't you going to apologize?"

"Apologize for what?"

She glared at him, but he scarcely noticed. She'd changed from her jeans into a soft pink dress that framed her dark prettiness, and he could barely keep his mind on their conversation.

"For accusing me of wanting to mistreat Terri. As if I would!"

He shrugged his shoulders, trying to force his thoughts back to his daughter. She'd talked a lot at dinner about Melissa Kennedy and the two little girls. He knew she'd like to go back over there again.

"She has chores to do."

"Maybe you're the one who mistreats her," she challenged.

He leaped to his feet. She'd touched his sore spot.

"Ms. Kennedy, you can take your cookies and your softness and trot right back to your perfect house. I don't need some do-gooder telling me how to raise my daughter!"

She rose to stand in front of him, almost nose to nose, except she was shorter than him. "All I'm trying to do is help three little girls be happy! Don't you care about Terri's happiness?"

"Of course I do!" he yelled. "I love my daughter!"

"Then how can you condemn her to sit in this house all alone for the rest of the summer? Even you, a hardheaded male, can see how unhappy she would be."

"A hardheaded—" he sputtered, unable to finish.

"What would it hurt for your daughter to spend some time with us?" Her voice softened and she added, "I promise she'll enjoy herself."

The difficulty was, he'd already realized Terri was going to be bored. And he hadn't known what to do about it. Now he was being offered a solution, but he didn't want to accept it. He didn't want his daughter falling into the trap of thinking she had a...a...a mother figure.

Once before, a woman had courted him through Terri. His daughter had been badly hurt when things hadn't worked out.

"That's what I'm afraid of," he muttered.

"What?" Melissa asked, leaning closer to him.

He stepped back. "Three hours a day?"

Her face brightened, as she realized she'd won. He backed up again. There was so much warmth coming from her, he figured a man would never be cold around her.

"She could come for lunch every day. There's no point in her having to fix a meal for herself when it's so easy to add one to our lunch. Then, I'll make sure she's home by four. Will that be okay?"

She was practically bouncing on her toes, beaming at him. Lord have mercy, what had he done?

Chapter Two

Rob told Terri the news the next morning over breakfast.

His daughter launched herself at him, wrapping her hands around his neck. "Oh, Daddy, thank you!"

Emotion rocked his heart. She seldom called him "Daddy" anymore, not since she thought she was growing up. "Listen to me, little girl," he began sternly. "This is a job. I'm not letting this woman adopt you. Understand?"

Terri continued to beam at him, as if he hadn't spoken. "Of course not, Dad. When do I go?"

"She said come to lunch. But you're to be back here at four, and you do your chores in the morning before you go."

"Yes, Dad." Her dutiful response was still accompanied by a huge smile.

Did that mean he'd done the right thing? Sometimes, as a parent, he felt lost. Before his father died, he'd at least had someone to discuss his decisions with.

The three of them, his father, him and Terri, had lived on the family ranch in south Texas. It had been home, even if it wasn't highly successful. His father had been reluctant to change anything.

When his father died, the taxes on the ranch, already cash-poor, had made it impossible to keep. He'd had to sell out to a neighbor.

Unable to bear watching someone else implement the changes he'd wanted to make, he'd decided it was time for him and his daughter to move on.

He'd put away the money left over from the sale and promised himself he'd own his own place again...someday.

He'd worried that the move, after just losing her grandfather, had been too hard on Terri. He'd worried that she wouldn't make new friends. He'd worried about her having to start a new school. He'd worried about her being alone all day while he worked.

Now he had that last problem solved.

So, instead, he worried all day about his daughter.

Melissa's suddenly conceived plan of having Terri help her was a brilliant success. Jessica and Mary Ann followed the older girl around like little puppies. Terri was affectionate and caring.

Her father had done a good job of raising her, Melissa decided. She was sweet, gentle and agreeable.

"Where's your mother?" Melissa asked over an afternoon snack.

Terri seemed unconcerned about the question. "She left when I was a baby. Dad says she wanted to be a big movie star."

"Oh, I'm sorry," Melissa quickly apologized.

"It's okay. Me and Dad and Grandpa did fine."

"Our mama left us," Jessica whispered, as if she feared her words would shock everyone.

For the first time, Terri seemed upset. Not about her own abandonment, but about Jessica and Mary Ann's. She looked at Melissa, as the younger girls did.

"We know, Jessica, and we're sorry, but we're lucky, too." Melissa smiled as all three girls stared at her, perplexed.

"How?" Terri asked.

"Because we get to be together. I never would've met Jessica and Mary Ann if they hadn't been left behind. And you wouldn't be here with us, either."

Melissa turned the situation into a celebration that the little girls joined in. Terri sent her a congratulatory smile, as if she understood, and they all toasted their togetherness with a lifting of their milk glasses.

After Terri left, promptly at four, Melissa stood watching the young girl walk to her house and thought again of the gruff man from last night.

He might not be friendly to her, but he loved his daughter. In spite of not wanting Terri to spend time with her, Rob Hanson had agreed because it was best for Terri. So, for what it was worth, Rob Hanson received Melissa Kennedy's stamp of approval.

As if he'd care.

She giggled at the thought. She could just picture

the look of disgust on his face if she told him. He wouldn't be impressed.

It didn't matter. Unlike Jessica and Mary Ann's parents, Rob Hanson hadn't abandoned his daughter, even though she'd only been a baby when his wife had left them. Admiration filled her. He'd cared for his daughter when another man might've given up. And he'd done an excellent job.

She didn't care if he didn't want her opinion. She intended to tell him the next time she saw him what a good parent he was.

Rob didn't get home until almost seven. He was tired, hungry, and worried. As he stepped onto the porch, the door swung open and Terri's happy face greeted him.

"Dad!" She offered him a kiss on the cheek, a fairly unusual occurrence, which reflected her mood. Then she protested, "Eew! You smell."

He cocked one brow. "No more than normal. Give me five minutes and I'll clean up."

After a quick shower and clean clothes, he returned to the kitchen, surprised by the delicious smells. For a twelve-year-old, Terri did a good job of throwing something together for dinner. But her efforts didn't involve much actual cooking.

He watched as she carefully removed a casserole of some kind from the oven and placed it on the table. "You cooked?" he asked abruptly.

She beamed at him. "Melissa taught me. We made this casserole together."

Before he could comment, she put a pan of rolls

in the oven. Then she opened the refrigerator and withdrew a tossed salad.

He took a long drink from the iced tea she'd already placed on the table. Suddenly he noticed a complete place setting of utensils. Usually, she only put out a fork for each of them.

"How come we're getting all fancied up suddenly?" he growled.

His heart sank as Terri stared at him, dismay in her gaze. "Don't you like it? Everything's so nice at Melissa's, I thought I'd try to do better here."

He took the napkin from beside his plate and spread it in his lap. "Sure I like it, baby," he agreed heartily, hoping to erase that look from her face. "And the food smells great."

She forgave his momentary criticism and soon they were eating. He'd worked hard all day, with only a brief break for a packed lunch. He was starving.

But he had to eat his meal with a constant stream of praises for Melissa Kennedy. Terri had had a wonderful day, it appeared. His worry had been for nothing.

Now he was really worried.

He knew he was right when Terri brought out half a chocolate cake.

"You baked half a cake?" he teased.

"No, silly. Melissa said she was glad to have someone to share a cake with. It would ruin before they could eat all of it, and that would be wasteful."

"That was kind of her," he muttered, and decided if he heard the fateful words "Melissa said" one more time, he'd throw the cake against the wall.

At least he would've until he tasted it.

He'd find something else to throw.

"Melissa said—"

"Terri!"

His unaccustomed snapping stopped his daughter in midsentence. "What, Dad? Don't you like the cake?"

With a sigh he said, "The cake is delicious. But could you possibly start a sentence with something other than 'Melissa said'?"

Her eyes rounded in surprise. Then hurt. "Sorry," she muttered. And said nothing else.

The change from constant chatter to absolute silence was unnerving. Rob tried several topics of conversation, but Terri didn't respond.

Finally he gave up and stood to clear the table. Terri carried her own dishes to the sink. "I'll clean up," he said. "After all, you did the cooking tonight. It's only fair."

"Melissa—I mean, I didn't do much."

He put an arm around his daughter and kissed her forehead. "I'm sorry I was an old grump, baby. I'm glad you enjoyed your day."

His apology released a flood of words. While he washed the dishes, Terri told him again about her day, and how much she'd enjoyed being with the other females.

He frowned, feeling a little rejection.

As if sensing his feelings, Terri quickly added, "I didn't mean I don't like being with you, Dad. But Melissa—she knows so much about girl things."

"Yeah." Terri was right about that. Melissa Kennedy knew how to make a man ache. To make a man want. And he didn't want to do either of those things.

A knock on the door disturbed them.

Terri hurried to answer it and reappeared in the kitchen a couple of minutes later with the one person he didn't want to see.

Melissa Kennedy, accompanied by the two little girls.

"Good evening. I hope you don't mind our visit," she said with a smile as she entered.

"After that dinner, I could hardly object, now, could I?"

He'd meant to sound like he was teasing her and thanking her at the same time. Unfortunately, his voice had come out harsh.

She stiffened, apparently not fooled by the awkward smile he attached to the end of his words. "I'm sorry for the intrusion, but the girls wanted to see where Terri lived."

Terri looked from him to Melissa and back again. Damn, he was going to be in trouble with his daughter if he didn't do a better job. "No problem. Have a seat. I'll be finished here in a minute."

"Dad, can I show the girls my bedroom?" Terri asked. "I told them about my dolls and they want to see them."

"Sure."

He stubbornly continued to wash the dishes as the children left the room, reluctant to acknowledge that he was alone with Melissa.

But she didn't sit down at the table. Instead he suddenly found her beside him, the cup towel Terri had been using in her hands.

"You don't have to do that."

"I know, but I'm more comfortable when I'm busy." She picked up a plate and dried it. "Where do they go?"

He nodded to the cabinet in front of her. "Up there."

She put the plate inside and picked up the other one. He scrubbed extra hard on the almost-clean Pyrex dish that had held the casserole.

"I have something to tell you."

His head whipped around to stare at the beautiful woman beside him. Tonight her dress was mint-green, almost the color of her eyes. It fit snugly from the waist up, and he hurriedly looked away. "Yeah?"

"You're a good father."

He dropped the dish. Fortunately, the water cushioned its landing so it didn't break. It only splashed him with water. Melissa took the cup towel and began blotting his shirt. He thought he'd die.

Melissa felt the hard muscles of his chest and stomach beneath the cup towel. Her mouth went dry. The man was like a rock. Visions of what he'd look like without the shirt filled her head, and she found herself staring into his blue eyes.

"Why did you say that?" he demanded harshly.

She took a step back. He sounded like a lion. "I— when I met you yesterday, I thought...you seemed hard." Her face turned bright red. She had ample proof that he was hard, but that wasn't what she had meant. "I wanted you to know that Terri is a special little girl. And since you're the one who raised her, it's obvious you did a good job.''

Seemingly reluctantly, he muttered, "Thanks."

"Do you want me to dry your shirt more?" she asked, her breathing getting more shallow as she both feared and wanted to help him.

"No! No, it doesn't matter." He took the cup towel from her hands, however, and rubbed it against his shirt.

Her gaze was fixed on the motion of his hand. When it stopped moving, she looked up to find his blue eyes fixed on her face. More specifically, on her lips.

As if he intended to kiss her.

She thought she stopped breathing altogether.

The girls tumbling back into the room, happiness exuding from them, broke the tension of the moment.

"Melissa, Terri's got three dollies!" Jessica announced with awe. Mary Anne nodded emphatically, holding up three fingers.

"Really? How wonderful. May I see?" she asked, anxious to escape Rob's presence.

Terri eagerly led Melissa from the room. The two little girls, realizing they would be left with Terri's dad, chased after them, calling for them to wait.

When they returned to the kitchen, the sink was empty and Rob was gone.

Melissa discarded the disappointment that filled her as ridiculous. "Um, I was going to ask your dad about a shopping trip tomorrow."

"Shopping?" Terri asked, her eyes widening with excitement. "Where?"

"There's a big mall in Wichita Falls that has everything. I need to buy things for the girls, and I thought you might need to shop, too.''

Without another word to her, Terri headed for the door, shouting for her father. When she got an answer, she turned to Melissa. ''I think he's outside. Come on.''

Melissa and the little girls followed her outside. Rob Hanson was sitting on the porch steps, his back to them.

''Dad, Melissa has something to ask you,'' Terri told him in a rush of words.

Melissa watched as the man stood. He was so tall and strong, so...overpowering. She inhaled a deep breath and took a step forward, feeling the younger girls pressing against her legs, as if for protection.

''Mr. Hanson, I'm taking the girls into Wichita Falls tomorrow to shop for some clothes. I thought maybe Terri would like to go with us. She would be a big help.''

''Please, Dad, please,'' Terri added almost before Melissa stopped speaking. ''I have my birthday money, and I really need some new things. I've outgrown everything!''

His frown didn't look like approval to Melissa. Surely the man would understand his daughter's need to—

''Sure, baby, you can go. We probably need some things for the house, too, since we didn't bring that much.''

Melissa swallowed, not sure she should speak. But she did. ''I talked to Abby earlier. She said if you needed to go with us, she could spare you one day.''

He jerked his head around to stare at her. ''Go

with you? I can't take off work to shop! That's ridiculous."

Melissa figured she might as well go all the way. "She also said you could have an advance on your salary if you needed it."

He took a menacing step toward her. "I don't need charity."

"No one offered you charity," she assured him, her voice cold. "You'll earn every penny Abby pays you. Ranch work is hard." Like his body. She banished that thought at once.

"Dad, it would be so great. If you came, I could get a bedspread and maybe some place mats, like Melissa has. We could have a real home."

Melissa knew nothing of their circumstances. Terri had mentioned her grandfather dying recently, but that was all. She watched Rob's face in the stream of light from the kitchen. Clearly he was struggling with his decision.

"Tell you what, baby, why don't you and I go shopping tomorrow evening? We can eat out, make a night of it."

He put a heartiness into his words, to convince his daughter, but Melissa suspected Terri could hear the reluctance as easily as she could.

To Melissa's surprise, instead of accepting his offer, Terri turned a bright red and stared down at the porch. "Dad, there's something...I need Melissa's help."

"You can pick out place mats as well as she can," he assured his daughter.

Terri grew even more embarrassed. Melissa

stepped closer to the young girl. She wasn't sure what was going on, but she wanted to help.

"I need Melissa," Terri said firmly, but she didn't meet her father's gaze.

He turned to glare at Melissa, as if his daughter's defection was her fault.

She leaned closer to Terri. "What is it?" she said softly.

Terri leaned over and whispered her problem in Melissa's ear.

Melissa bit her bottom lip, knowing the man towering over her was going to hate what she had to tell him. "Terri, why don't you walk the girls back to the house and get them started on their baths. Your dad and I will be there in a second."

"Are you sure?" Terri asked, her gaze darting between her dad and Melissa.

"I'm sure, honey. Everything will be fine."

Terri looked at her dad again, then took the little girls' hands and hurried around him and down the steps.

Melissa stood waiting until the children were out of earshot. Rob didn't move, either, until they heard the door closing at Melissa's house.

"My daughter and I don't have secrets," he growled in a low voice.

"It's not a secret, Rob. But Terri finds it a little embarrassing to explain it to you." She figured it was going to be a little embarrassing for her, too, but she was a mature adult.

"What is it?"

"Terri needs some new underwear."

"Hell, I've bought her underwear before. I don't

know why that would embarrass her. Did you put some silly ideas in her head? Is that why—''

"She needs a bra."

Her words stopped his sputtering stone cold.

Chapter Three

Rob stared at Melissa, speechless. A bra? His little girl needed a bra? No! She was only...twelve, almost thirteen. Almost a teenager.

"But she can't...she's too...what do I do?" He realized his mistake at once. He'd appeared vulnerable in front of Melissa. He stepped back as she moved forward.

"Rob, it's not that big a deal. If you go with us tomorrow, you can take the little ones for ice cream while Terri and I make a quick purchase. After once or twice, she'll be able to shop by herself, if she needs to."

He should've been relieved. But he'd heard all she hadn't said. She expected him to go on a shopping trip in the middle of the week with her and three children. She expected him to take the two little ones for ice cream. Most important of all, she expected him to act like a husband.

"I can't do that!" he returned harshly.

"Okay." Without waiting for an answer, she stepped around him, down the steps, and walked toward her house.

"Wait!" he called, hurrying after her. She never broke stride, however, until he grabbed her arm. "What do you mean, okay?"

"If you can't go, you can't go. I hope Terri can still go."

"Of course she can. But what about…I mean—"

"Terri purchasing her underwear? If we can't manage it with the other two children, I guess you'll have to take her shopping for it. After all, she's your child."

She pulled free and began walking again.

It was a warm night. But the sweat beads on his forehead were from nerves, not the summer air. He'd walked past stores like Victoria's Secret, but he'd always looked the other way. He'd ordered Terri's undergarments from the Sears catalog. He'd never actually been in a lingerie department.

Melissa had said Terri could learn to shop for these things without any help.

He licked his dry lips. In the interest of being independent of Melissa Kennedy in the future, he needed to see that Terri got the instruction she needed.

He could do this.

"I-if Abby doesn't mind, I'll go tomorrow. You'll show Terri how—I mean, you'll help her?"

"Of course. I'll be glad to. And the girls love ice cream, so they'll be good for you. They haven't gotten ten many treats in their little lives."

He frowned at the sadness of her words, but he still hadn't dealt with all the plans for tomorrow. "What time will we leave in the morning?"

"I thought we should leave about nine-fifteen. The stores don't open until ten."

"Then I'll have time to talk to Abby in the morning. You're sure she said it would be okay?"

"I wouldn't lie to you, Rob. She knew you started work at once. Sometimes it takes people a little longer to get settled."

"I can do a few chores before we leave," he figured aloud. He usually started his day at six.

They'd reached her front porch, its light shining in the night. The smile on her face didn't look condescending, but he wasn't sure. "Will you send Terri out?"

"Of course, but you're welcome to come in to wait for her. I'll have to go upstairs to get her. We can't leave the little ones in the bath without someone to watch them."

"No, I'll wait here."

"Then, I'll see you in the morning," she said, still smiling. He watched until the door closed behind her. Then he sank down onto the porch steps. She had a Mona Lisa smile if he'd ever seen one. But she was a hell of a lot sexier than that Italian lady.

Didn't mean he could figure her out.

But that didn't matter. He was getting some help for Terri. He guessed he'd have to admit that she was getting to the age that he couldn't fix everything for her.

He should be grateful there was a woman nearby who could help her. But he should've asked Ellen to help. She was nice, motherly. She didn't get him all hot and bothered.

He would've asked her, if he'd known there was a problem. But Terri had blindsided him tonight. She hadn't talked to him. She hadn't asked for help. At least, not from him.

That hurt.

But then, he couldn't help her pick out a bra. So maybe it was just as well she hadn't asked him. But if she had, he could've asked Ellen.

Oh, hell!

Rob administered the medicine to the two horses in the barn, feeding and watering them, too. Then he checked his list for any last-minute chores to do before he cleaned up. He'd talked to Abby just after breakfast. She'd assured him they could make it one day without him.

With a shrug of his shoulders, he turned back to the house where he and Terri had moved. It wasn't a bad place. Ellen had helped them clean it up.

If it made Terri happy to buy a few things, dress it up a little, he'd agree to that. But he needed to get it all done today. He didn't intend to take another day off just to go shopping.

His daughter was waiting in the kitchen, her dark hair, the same color as his, gleaming, curled under around her heart-shaped face.

"You look pretty, baby."

"Thanks, Dad. Uh, could you not call me 'baby' when we're out? I'm more grown-up now, and…and I don't want people to think I'm still in elementary school."

"Right," he agreed, though he hated the idea. "I'll try to remember."

"Thanks, Dad," she said, a sweet smile on her face as she leaned over to kiss him. Then she pulled back. "Hurry. You smell like horses."

"Yes, ma'am," he agreed, and continued on to the bathroom. He wanted to get this chore over with as soon as possible.

After cleaning up, he gathered his billfold, checkbook and charge cards. He wasn't sure what he'd need, but from what he'd heard, he'd need something to pay the bills. Women and shopping could get out of hand.

When he returned to the kitchen, Terri was coming in the front door.

"Come on, Dad. Melissa's outside."

"Okay, okay. You got everything you need?"

"Yeah," she threw over her shoulder as she hurried out the door.

Melissa Kennedy was a damned pied piper. If she told Terri to jump off a cliff, he figured his kid would run over him to do just that.

He was frowning when he looked up and saw the Chevy Suburban parked out front. The vehicle was new. Melissa was standing beside the passenger door. Terri had already gotten in the back.

"Do you mind driving?" she asked, smiling again. "Me?"

"Aren't you comfortable driving? I thought it would be easier for me to deal with the girls, if they get nervous, if you're driving." When he didn't say anything, she added, "I can drive, though, if—"

"I'll drive."

He pulled open the passenger door and waited until she got in. Then he closed it and circled the vehicle to slide behind the wheel. He was comfortable driving. But little girls didn't bother him, either. After all, he'd raised Terri.

Melissa gave him brief, succinct directions, and he looked at her in surprise. His experience said a woman couldn't tell you how to go in a straight line without a lot of side trips.

Abby Kennedy had been direct, he had to admit. Maybe Melissa had something in common with her sister, after all.

Which made him wonder about the third sister.

"I haven't met your other sister," he said, staring ahead of him as he drove.

"She and her husband have been attending the rodeo in Oklahoma City. They'll be back on Monday."

He looked at her. "They follow the rodeos?"

"Not full-time, but Jed's been training some guys, and he wanted to see how they do."

"Who's Jed?"

"Jed Davis, Beth's husband."

He almost stopped the truck. "Your sister is married to Jed Davis?"

"Yes, do you know him?"

"We've met. He's the best there is as a trainer." He'd heard that Davis had settled down somewhere in Texas, but he hadn't realized it was here.

"Yes, he's good."

One of the children claimed her attention at that moment, and Rob didn't speak again until they reached the mall. He'd been afraid things would be awkward this morning, but Melissa was easy to talk to. He was going to have to watch himself.

"Okay," he said with a sigh, "how do we do this? Do I take them for ice cream at once? Or—"

Both Terri and Melissa looked at him as if he'd offered to run them over to Mars.

"No. We have an entire list of things to buy," Melissa assured him. "This is an all-day project."

"All day?" Rob gasped in surprise. He figured he'd get in an afternoon's work when they got back home. "Surely no more than a couple of hours." He must've misunderstood.

"I'm sorry. I thought you realized we probably wouldn't go back home until suppertime."

"Yeah, Dad, it takes a while to shop," Terri added, glaring at him.

"Okay," he said in resignation. "What do I do?"

Melissa seemed more understanding than Terri. She smiled. "The first thing we're going to buy are two umbrella strollers."

"I think Terri's too old for a stroller," he said, hoping to put a smile on his daughter's face.

"Dad!" she protested.

Melissa said, "I think your dad is teasing you, sweetie. He knows I meant them for Jessica and Mary Ann."

"Even they seem a little old for strollers," he pointed out. After all, they walked just fine.

"If we were only going to be a few minutes, you'd be right. But in an hour, they'll both be tired and want to be carried. It will be easier with a stroller."

He bowed to her greater knowledge. And discovered she was right. An added benefit was that they were belted in and couldn't run away. Or get lost.

After an hour of shopping, he carried quite a few packages and Melissa and Terri pushed the little girls.

"Maybe I should go make a run to the car and dump these packages?"

"Oh, Rob, that would be great," Melissa said, her smile approving.

The pleasure that filled him at doing something she appreciated almost took control before he realized the danger. He frowned. "Where do I meet you?"

"Are you sure you don't mind?"

"I'm sure."

"We'll go into housewares and see if Terri can find some place mats she likes. Unless you want to pick them out?"

"No. Whatever she likes." And he hurried away.

"Your father doesn't seem happy," Melissa said, watching him weave his way between the few shoppers. The mall was always crowded on the weekends, but during the week it didn't do that much business.

"He's been grumpy lately. I think he hated having to sell the ranch." Terri spoke as she walked toward the store.

Melissa told herself not to pump the child for information, but one question didn't seem so awful. "You had to sell your ranch? I didn't know you had one."

"Yeah. It was Grandpa's. Dad said the taxes were too much, so we had to sell."

"Oh, I'm sorry." A lot of farm and ranch families

had that problem, but there were ways to avoid it if a good lawyer set up a trust. "Where was your ranch?"

"In south Texas near the border."

"Oh. That's a long way away."

"Yeah. But I like it here a lot better. We didn't have anyone else on the ranch but one cowboy. I got lonesome."

"I'm glad you're here, too. Let's go see what they have here for your new home, and then we'll break for lunch. Maybe that will cheer your father up."

He did appear a lot happier as he wolfed down a big thick hamburger with all the trimmings. The little girls stared at him, seemingly fascinated with his appetite.

"What's the matter?" he asked abruptly, putting down his hamburger and leaning toward Melissa, speaking in a whisper.

Melissa looked up. "What?"

"I don't know. They keep staring at me."

She probably should've filled Rob in on what she suspected about the children, but there really hadn't been an opportunity. Keeping her voice low, where the children wouldn't overhear, she said, "Um, I think their father wasn't…wasn't like you."

"In what way?"

"I don't think he liked children."

"His own children?" Rob asked in quiet horror. Melissa didn't want him to alarm the children, but she loved his reaction.

"Some men are that way," she said, shrugging off her answer.

"None that I know," he returned, glaring at her.

"It would probably be good if you smiled some," she whispered, nodding toward Jessica and Mary Ann.

He turned to look at the girls and actually gave them a charming smile, one that had Melissa's attention, too. Then he picked up a French fry and handed it to Jessica. "Want to try one? They're good."

Shock registered on Jessica's face. Then she cautiously reached for the fry, as if she expected him to snatch it back. Once she'd accepted it, he repeated the process to Mary Ann.

"We should've ordered them fries," he said with a frown.

"Smile," she reminded him.

Both girls had finished their fries by then and were again solemnly watching him.

Without consulting Melissa, he flagged down their waiter and asked for another order of fries and two saucers. Then he gave the girls each another piece of potato. "He's going to bring you some fries," he assured them, "but I'll share until yours arrive."

"Dad's good with kids," Terri said under her breath to Melissa.

"Yes, he is," she agreed. She'd already decided he was a good parent. His kindness to Jessica and Mary Ann meant a lot to Melissa. The girls needed to know that all men were not like their father.

Lunch was a big success until the waiter brought the bill. Melissa reached for it, but Rob was faster. "What are you doing?" she asked. "This is my treat."

"You paid for the gasoline," he said calmly, taking out several bills and leaving them on the table with the tab.

"But you can't—"

"Ready, girls?" he asked, standing, ignoring her protest.

"Rob, this isn't necessary. I'll—"

He took her arm, as if he were escorting her out of the restaurant, and leaned close to her ear. "Melissa, I'm trying to be reasonable about today, but I do not eat and let a lady pay. You'll just have to accept that."

Then he buckled the two girls into their strollers, indicated Terri should take one, and he pushed the other out of the restaurant.

Melissa, still rooted by the table, stared after him.

"Is everything all right, miss?" the waiter asked.

"Oh! Yes, everything is fine." She hurried after the others.

But she was going to have to be on her toes. This man was too sweet…and too macho. Her few experiences with men had not been happy ones. They weren't interested in raising someone else's children.

And she had no intention of letting anyone, even a sexy, caring cowboy, take away her dream.

Because she worried about the little girls being left alone with Rob, Melissa decided they should all go to the ice-cream store. Then, once the girls were eating their ice cream, she and Terri would slip away.

The plan worked beautifully. Jessica and Mary Ann loved ice cream. Rob left them in their strollers and fed both of them from a big cup.

"We'll hurry," Melissa assured them.

"No problem. We've got things under control. Terri, here's some extra money if you need it," he said, handing his daughter some folded dollars.

"I have my birthday money, Dad," she told him.

"Birthday money should be spent on something fun, not for, uh, things you need."

They started to walk away, but he called Melissa back. "If she sees some jeans, shirts, things like that, you might help her choose some. She's outgrown those jeans she's wearing."

Melissa smiled. Terri's jeans were skintight. Rob was apparently getting into the spirit of shopping. With a nod, she and Terri set out to shop till they dropped.

When she realized how long they'd been gone, a little over an hour later, she hurried them back to the ice-cream store, feeling very guilty. Their hands were full of packages, having found the proper underwear and five outfits, most of them on sale.

She was amazed at the patience on Rob's face. He was still sitting at the corner table. The little girls, strapped in their strollers, were sound asleep.

"I'm so sorry," she whispered as she sat down beside him. "I didn't intend to stay gone so long, but we—"

"Oh, Dad, wait until you see what I bought!" Terri said eagerly, starting to open some of the packages.

Rob turned red in the face. "Not here!" he protested hoarsely.

Melissa knew what he'd thought. She hurriedly reassured him. "I think she wants to show you her new jeans and T-shirts and shorts."

"Oh!"

"Dad!" Terri protested, now as red as her father.

"Sorry, baby—I mean, Terri. I wasn't thinking."

Melissa watched father and daughter as she showed him her purchases, well, most of them, and he patiently listened and praised her choices.

She knew he wasn't perfect, but he was the perfect father. Every little girl should have a father like him. Her own father had been pretty special, but he'd died in a car crash with her mother when Melissa was ten.

Sometimes she longed for those times when he'd held her in his arms, and she'd felt so safe, so loved. She blinked back tears, surprised at how moved she was.

"What's wrong?" Rob asked under his breath, leaning toward her.

"Nothing. I was thinking about…about something sad. I'm glad you like her choices. Terri has great taste."

"Yeah," he agreed, but he kept his gaze on her face, and she hoped her tears dried up quickly. She'd be so embarrassed if he caught her crying.

After a moment of silence he said, "So, are we finished?"

Melissa pursed her lips. "No. There's one more thing I want to buy. Neither girl has any kind of doll or toy. I want to buy them each a doll. Or a stuffed bear."

A smile that completely melted her heart spread across Rob's face. "Melissa Kennedy, I think you have too soft a heart for the job you're trying to do."

"Why do you say that?"

"Because you're already in love with those kids.

How are you going to feel when they take them away?''

"Take them away?" Terri cried. "What are you talking about?"

Melissa caught the chagrined expression on Rob's face before she turned to Terri. "Honey, I told you I'm their foster mother. That means I provide care for them until…until they're adopted or their parents are located."

"No!" Jessica cried, apparently having awakened in time to hear Melissa. She fought to get out of her stroller. "No, I don't want Daddy to come back!"

Mary Ann started crying.

Before Melissa could move, Rob had unbelted Jessica and lifted her into his lap. "It's okay, little one. You're safe. We're taking care of you."

Melissa did the same for Mary Ann, settling her down, too. Terri looked on helplessly, her gaze filled with concern.

Melissa held the warm little body against her, cuddling Mary Ann, staring at Rob. For a tough cowboy, he had a sensitive side that impressed her.

A tough, sexy cowboy who made the perfect father.

Chapter Four

Rob's perfection only lasted about half an hour.

By the time they'd bought the dolls and returned to the Suburban, he was the gruff, unfriendly cowboy she'd first met. He scarcely spoke to her, and when he did, it came out as a growl. He ignored the children.

Melissa wanted to grab him by his collar and shake him. She wanted to demand to know what was wrong. She wanted to give him a swift kick in his rear.

Of course, she did none of those things.

"I appreciate your going with us today. We got a great deal accomplished." She shot him her sweetest smile.

He frowned and said nothing.

"I think Terri chose some nice things."

Nothing.

"Thank you for buying lunch. I didn't intend for you to do that."

Complete silence.

Finally, her frustration reached the boiling point. "Have you gone deaf since we left the mall? Are you missing the excitement of shopping? We can go back tomorrow if you want."

"No thanks."

"Ah, he speaks," she announced to Terri, sitting right behind her father.

His daughter looked uneasy, and Melissa felt badly about bringing her father's bad mood to Terri's attention.

The rest of the way home, she talked to Terri and the little girls, ignoring the man beside her. Jessica and Mary Ann cuddled their choices against their thin chests as if they'd never let them go. Mary Ann had chosen a small Raggedy Ann, but Jessica had chosen a big bear. She spent the trip home practicing her growls, trying to scare Terri and Melissa with the ferocity of her play toy. Melissa wondered if the child had chosen the bear in hopes of finding protection.

When they reached the ranch, it was after six. Melissa cleared her throat and looked at the stern man beside her. "I have dinner ready, if you and Terri would like to join us. I imagine she's tired after shopping all day."

"How can you have dinner ready?" he asked, still frowning.

"I put it in a Crock-Pot before we left this morning. It will take about ten minutes to get everything on the table." She saw the no on his face before he could speak and added, "I can fix a plate for the two of you to take home, if you don't want to eat with us."

Apparently her gracious offer in the face of his rudeness got to him. His cheeks flushed and he looked away. "We'll be glad to eat with you. Thanks."

"Oh, good," Terri said with a sigh of relief. "'Cause I don't have anything fixed for supper."

Melissa smiled at her. "If you'll take the girls upstairs and tend to them, I'll put dinner on the table. We'll let your dad carry in all the packages."

"That may take a while," he said under his breath.

Melissa raised her chin. She wasn't going to be intimidated by this man. "Probably. Fortunately, you have strong muscles, so I think you can manage."

He glared at her and opened his car door. Once he was out of her eyesight, she organized the children and got them in the house. Then she left the two little ones to Terri and hurried to the kitchen.

Putting on a pot of coffee first thing, she then dished up the meat and vegetables from the Crock-Pot. She'd prepared a salad, except for the dressing, which she now added. Then she took the apple pie she'd made for dessert from the refrigerator and put it in the oven to warm.

She stepped to the hallway to call everyone to dinner, only to find Rob standing amid a pile of packages.

"I didn't know where to put them," he said, shrugging his massive shoulders.

"That's fine. Dinner is ready." She turned toward

the stairs and shouted to Terri, then went back into the kitchen.

Rob followed.

"It's hard to believe you could do all this so quickly," he said, frowning again.

"It just takes planning. Would you pour some milk for the children?" she asked, setting out three glasses on the counter.

By the time he'd poured the milk and she'd fixed iced tea for the two adults, Terri, Jessica and Mary Ann had come down. Silence fell while they ate. Shopping made for good appetites.

When she pulled the apple pie out of the oven, Rob stared at her. "You made that after we got home?"

"No, I made it last night and put it in the refrigerator. I've only heated it up."

Terri took the girls upstairs to read them a good-night story as soon as they'd finished eating. Melissa figured they'd fall asleep before she finished the first page.

She poured Rob a cup of coffee.

"Would you like another piece of pie?"

"I don't want to look like a pig," he muttered, but his gaze lingered on the remains of the pie.

She'd missed cooking for a hardworking man since she'd moved to her new house. Rob's appreciation for her cooking was nice. She cut him another piece and slid it onto his plate.

"I'm going to have to go twice as hard tomorrow to work this off," he said just before he took a huge bite.

"I doubt that," she said, her gaze roving over his

body. There were no signs of overindulgence. She turned bright red when her gaze collided with his.

After he'd finished his second piece, he cleared his throat and Melissa braced for what was coming.

"I want to thank you for helping Terri. I hadn't—it's hard to realize she's growing up. I appreciate it."

"But you don't want to do it again anytime soon?" she teased, unable to resist.

He looked alarmed. "You said she could manage on her own now."

"She probably can. But it's good for her to have female friends."

"I know that."

He was back to growling.

"Are you going to church on Sunday?"

"You in charge of feeding my soul as well as my body?" he asked, his mouth turned down.

"No, but I thought I might introduce Terri to some of the kids her age. The sooner she makes friends, the happier she'll be." She watched him as he realized he'd been rude again.

"Sorry. That'll be nice."

Terri entered the kitchen. "They're both asleep, clutching their presents."

"Thanks so much, Terri. You've been terrific today," Melissa assured her, standing and crossing the kitchen to give the girl a hug.

Terri returned the hug enthusiastically. "I had the best time."

"Good. Your dad said the two of you would come to church on Sunday and I can introduce you to some of the kids you'll be in school with."

"Wow! Thanks, Melissa," Terri said, hugging Melissa again.

Rob glared at Melissa over Terri's head.

"Let's go home," he said abruptly. "Shopping tires me out."

Melissa watched him walk away from her house, his arms full of Terri's packages. He was still a good father, but not a perfect man. Unless you considered his muscles.

She shut away that thought at once.

Rob started early and worked late the next few days, determined to erase any memory of Melissa. He didn't see her at all, but he heard about her. His daughter chattered away each evening as they ate, assuring him of Melissa's influence. He couldn't complain. He was eating better food, usually prepared by Melissa. His daughter was happy. Even the house looked better.

All he could do was keep his distance.

Abby teased him about shopping with her sister, as did Floyd and Barney, the cowhands. Dirk, the third cowboy, never said much. Rob took their ribbing in stride, telling them shopping was worse than branding. They'd completed the spring roundup before he had been hired, so he didn't have to worry about doing that job until fall.

He liked his work. He was satisfied at the end of the day when he trudged over to his house. The only fly in the ointment of his happiness was thoughts of Melissa. She was the ultimate "trap" for a single man. She was beautiful, pleasant and the perfect housekeeper.

He'd fallen for that once before. He knew what happened after the marriage vows. His wife had complained, wanted him to change, to take her to the city. Hell, what would he do in a city? She'd used sex to force him to change his behavior. She'd withheld food, too. She'd even gotten pregnant and tried to use the baby as a bargaining chip.

In the end, she'd left.

He and his dad had raised Terri together. Now his dad was gone, and he wasn't doing so well on his own. Which brought his thoughts back to Melissa.

He felt as though he were losing his little girl to Melissa's influence. He supposed he should be grateful she was a good woman. But Terri was *his* child.

Saturday, he was helping move one of the herds to a new pasture, when Abby got a call on her cellular phone. He didn't pay any attention to it because Ellen and Melissa called her several times a day. This time, however, she hung up and raced her horse around the herd to him.

"What's up?" he asked, frowning.

"A neighbor and his wife have been killed in a car wreck. I need to go see if I can do anything to help. Can you manage without me?"

"Sure. We'll be fine."

She scarcely waited for him to answer, urging her horse in the direction of the barn. He was glad Abby believed she could trust him.

That's how it was in small communities. If a tragedy happened, everyone pitched in to help. When his father had died, the ladies had brought in enough food to feed an army. That was one of the reasons he'd refused to move to a city.

Yes, he was perfectly content with being on the ranch with his daughter. *And Melissa,* a small voice inside his head said. He decided to ignore it.

"Mr. Graham, you can't do this!" Melissa said insistently, fighting the tears in her eyes.

The head of Social Services, Charles Graham, shook his head. "Now, Melissa, you've already got two children. Besides, two of the three children are boys."

"I have plenty of room for three more," she assured him. "And what difference does it make if they're boys?"

She and Abby had gotten to the Prine Ranch a couple of hours ago. Larry and Julia Prine, the owners, had been killed in a car wreck just this morning. They left behind three children, Wayne, thirteen, Billy, nine, and Susan, six.

Since it was a replay of the tragedy Melissa and her sisters had suffered, she knew how hard it would be for the three children to be split up, as Charles Graham was planning to do.

"Now, Melissa, we talked about this," he said, lowering his voice so the neighbors who'd come to offer assistance wouldn't overhear. "I don't think you should have charge of boys. They're different from girls. I want to place them with a married couple."

She and Abby exchanged a look of outrage and hysterical humor. What did the man think, that she'd crawled out from under a log last week? "I know that. But you can't split them up. It would be devastating."

"I don't have a choice. No one can take all three."

"But *I* can!" Abby's cautionary look told her she was almost screaming, and she struggled to bring herself under control as she tried to find a way to fix the situation.

"Yes, but you have no man in the house. I really believe—"

Suddenly Melissa remembered Rob Hanson. Without giving herself time to think things through, she grabbed Mr. Graham's arm. "What if— I'm engaged, Mr. Graham. My fiancé is around all the time, and we're going to be married soon."

"Engaged?" the man asked, his eyebrows soaring. "I hadn't heard that. Who's the lucky man?"

She avoided Abby's stare and said, "Rob Hanson."

"Don't know the man."

Melissa used her most charming smile. "He's new to the area. He's very good with kids. He has a twelve-year-old daughter, very well-behaved."

"You're to be married soon?"

Melissa swallowed and shot a side glance to her sister who was standing silently beside her. "Yes, within the month."

"That soon? Hmm, well, that does change things. He won't mind you taking in three more children?"

"Oh, no, not at all. He loves children."

"What's he do for a living?"

"He's Abby's foreman."

The man grinned. "I guess I don't have to worry about him losing his job, then, do I? Abby wouldn't fire her brother-in-law."

"Actually, I would, if he couldn't do the job,"

Abby said calmly, causing Melissa to gulp. "Fortunately, Rob is great at his job, and a hard worker."

Charles Graham stared at both of them for a minute. Then he said, "All right, I'll let you take them home with you, Melissa, temporarily. But I'm going to keep an eye on the situation. This isn't permanent."

Melissa could've kissed the man. She figured once she got the kids to her place, she'd find a way to keep them. They didn't appear to have any relatives other than a great-aunt in Dallas who was ninety-two and living in a nursing home.

"Thank you!" Then she excused herself, intent on hurrying to the kitchen where the children were.

Abby, however, halted her by grabbing her arm. "What is going on?" she whispered.

"I—I have a plan. I'll explain later," she hurriedly said, trusting her sister to keep silent until they could talk. And hoping Abby wouldn't condemn her impulsiveness.

Wayne, the oldest boy, had been trying to console his siblings and greet the well-wishers who had been arriving in a steady stream.

Melissa's heart went out to the boy as he stood there, his arms around his brother and sister, fighting the tears. She approached them. "Wayne, Mr. Graham has agreed that you and your brother and sister can come stay with me until everything gets straightened out."

"We can stay together, all three of us?" he asked.

"Yes, all together. I have two little girls living with me already, but there's plenty of room."

"You're not foolin' us?" The intensity of the

boy's face told Melissa how important it was to him. She remembered.

"Nope. I'm not. Why don't the three of you go pack a few clothes and anything else you think you might need. You can go home with me tonight. We'll come back over in a few days to...to take care of everything."

"What about the ranch? The animals?"

"Who's your foreman?"

"Didn't have one," Wayne said, fighting back tears. "Me and Dad and Billy did most of the work. Old Duffy helped out."

She looked over her shoulder and discovered Abby standing by the kitchen door. "I'll get Abby to talk to Duffy. Maybe he can manage to take care of everything for a little while. Go pack a few things."

Wayne shepherded his siblings from the room, and Melissa moved to Abby's side.

Her sister was waiting for her, a worried look on her face. "I think you need to explain about you and Rob. Have you two— Is it a secret?"

Melissa dropped her gaze. "It's so secret he doesn't know it, either."

Abby leaned closer. "Melissa Kennedy, are you telling me you lied to Mr. Graham?"

"I had to, Abby. He was going to split them up. You heard him. It would be terrible, just like with us."

"I know, I know," Abby said, patting her shoulder. "But isn't Rob going to object? I mean, have you—are you dating?"

"No! We're not anything. But he won't ever know. He hardly leaves the ranch, and who is Mr.

Graham going to tell? In a month or two, I'll explain that we broke up. He'll see how well the boys are doing, and he'll leave them with me.''

''I hope it works out that way.''

Melissa could hear doubt in her sister's voice, but she didn't care. Keeping the kids together, giving them a chance to heal, was important. ''Could you talk to Duffy about taking care of the animals for a little while? I don't know what will be done about the ranch, but Wayne is worried about the animals.''

''Sure. I'll see what we can do to help.''

When Rob came in for dinner that night, he learned about the new additions to Melissa's household. He figured that meant she wouldn't be going to church the next morning.

And he received another reminder that his daughter was growing up. She was sympathetic, of course, for the other children's loss. But she was also interested in Wayne Prine.

He stopped himself from pointing out that she was too young to be interested in boys. And he refrained from assuring her that romance only led to disaster. He nodded in sympathy and concentrated on his food.

''Dad, it's so sad. Susie is only six. I'm not sure she'll even remember her mom and dad,'' Terri told him.

''You don't remember your mom, and you turned out all right.''

''I know, but I had you and Grandpa. They lost both their parents.''

''But they'll have Melissa. She makes a pretty

good mom, doesn't she?" He thought she made a wonderful mother.

"Yes, but remember what she said about Jessie and Mary Ann? They could take them away if their parents came back." Terri appeared on the verge of tears and he reached out to catch her hand.

"Baby, you can't arrange life the way you want. Things happen. But they could get to stay with Melissa for a long time, couldn't they? So don't look for the worst to happen, okay?"

She sniffed and squeezed his hand. "That's what Melissa said, too."

He nodded.

"She said, I should try to smile a lot."

"That's a great idea. You have a wonderful smile."

She beamed at him. "Thanks, Dad. Do you mind if I don't get back to the house at four? Melissa is going to need a little more help. Since I don't have to cook dinner, I don't have much to do until you come home."

Rob frowned. "I don't want you to work too hard."

"It's not really work, Dad. I play with the little girls, that's all. Melissa does most of the work. Please?"

"Yeah, I guess so," he agreed, but it was with reluctance. He didn't want his daughter to get too wrapped up in a situation that could turn sad at any moment. "But tomorrow is Sunday. We're going to spend the day together cleaning here and finishing the unpacking. Okay?"

"Sure, Dad," she agreed, the picture of reasonableness.

Sunday was a day of rest for the cowboys, unless there were emergencies, after the animals were cared for. Rob justified his delaying going to church because of Melissa's preoccupation with the newly arrived Prine children.

Together he and Terri made a concentrated effort at settling in to their new home. Melissa's influence was everywhere, from Terri's chatter to the way she arranged their belongings.

Rob tried to ignore the fact that he was beginning to look forward to Melissa and her influence.

Monday morning, as he was leaving the table, Terri said, "I may go over to Melissa's a little early, if I get everything finished. So if you come home and I'm not here, just check with Melissa."

"But you said you were staying late. I don't want you spending your entire day over there," he protested.

"I won't, Dad. I'll get my chores done first."

With a sigh, he nodded and hurried to the barn. But his mind remained on the situation most of the morning. Melissa Kennedy was taking over his daughter's life, and, by remote control, his own.

He'd vowed to keep his distance from her when he'd realized how attractive she was to him. Not just physically, but her behavior, too. Her willingness to help children. Her smile.

He was going to have to work harder at resisting the attraction. He didn't intend to let himself fall into a woman's clutches again.

Ellen had packed lunches for all the hands since they were working far away from the ranch house. Abby wasn't with them, so Rob decided to have lunch with his men when they reached a small grove of trees that would provide shade for both them and their horses.

"Hot day, today," Floyd commented as he gave his horse a drink of water.

"Yeah," Rob agreed, his mind still on Melissa.

After they were all seated on the ground and taking out their food, Barney said, "I sure am glad Ellen is the cook. I didn't think they'd find anyone as good as Melissa, but Ellen is."

"Yeah," Floyd agreed.

Rob wasn't surprised with his agreement. Not only was Ellen a great cook, but everyone also knew she was the object of Floyd's affections.

"When are you and Ellen gettin' hitched?" Barney asked. "You ain't plannin' on taking her away, are you?"

"Nope. We're talking about it, but we haven't decided. I don't work as fast as some people."

Rob looked up in time to realize Floyd was staring at him. "What are you talking about?"

"I was surprised to find out how fast you are. Not that I don't like working for you, Rob, but Melissa is kind of special."

Uneasiness filled Rob. "I know that."

"You be good to her, you hear?"

"What are you talking about?" Rob demanded, tensing.

"I'm talking about you and Melissa being engaged."

Chapter Five

Rob's first instinct was to call Floyd a liar. But his father had taught him long ago not to fly off the handle. With all three men staring at him, he swallowed the food he was chewing.

Then he stared at Floyd. "Where did you hear that?"

"From Ellen. One of her friends was at the Prine place on Saturday, taking them food. She heard Melissa telling that Social Services guy that you was engaged and would be marryin' soon."

Something that hadn't seemed possible a minute ago now appeared plausible to Rob. Oh, not a real engagement, but a reason for the lie. It had to be somehow connected to the kids.

"Well, we aren't announcing anything yet." That was the best answer he could come up with until he talked to Melissa. And he definitely intended to talk to her.

But he couldn't leave the men unsupervised. Not that they wouldn't work, but they'd be suspicious of his leaving.

He finished his lunch, not bothering to enter into any more conversations. He didn't want to talk to anyone until he talked to Melissa Kennedy.

Terri had his dinner on the table when he got in that night, but she'd already eaten at Melissa's house. She joined him at the table, however, telling him about the events of her day.

"Melissa's thinking about getting some help to come in and clean twice a week. She says boys are just naturally messier than girls."

"She thinks these new ones will be staying?" He watched Terri's face, looking for any clues.

His daughter shrugged her shoulders, avoiding his gaze. "We all hope so. They're really nice. Wayne and I will be in the same class at school."

"They don't have any relatives to take them in?"

Terri shook her head. "Wayne said they had a great-aunt in Dallas, but she's around ninety." She said that age with awe that anyone could live that long. "Besides, Wayne said he couldn't live in a city."

That feeling struck a chord in Rob. Sympathy rose in him for Wayne Prine, but he also suspected he'd soon be tired of hearing "Wayne said," almost as he was of the "Melissa said" that his daughter used to start most sentences.

He rose and carried his plate to the sink. With his back to Terri, he said, "I need to talk to Melissa. What time do they all go to sleep?"

"The little girls are all probably asleep by now.

The two boys share a room and they get to read awhile. Why do you need to talk to Melissa?''

"It's adult stuff. You'll be okay here?"

"Can't I come with you?"

"Not if the other kids are in bed. Besides, I like that reading each evening. A good idea. You have a list of books you're supposed to read this summer."

"That was for my school back home," she hurriedly said.

"I don't think it will hurt you to read them, anyway. Don't you already have two or three of them?"

"Yes, but—"

"Good. Go get ready for bed. I'll wait until you're tucked in before I go see Melissa."

Terri left the kitchen, muttering under her breath about a dumb old rule. For the first time since Floyd's announcement, Rob smiled. At least his daughter wouldn't continue to think Melissa was perfect.

Half an hour later, he quietly shut the door behind him and strode the short distance to Melissa's house. The kitchen light was on, and he hoped that meant she was still up. Rapping softly on the door, he waited.

After a couple of minutes, he heard steps. The shutter beside the door opened, and he could make out Melissa's profile. Then the door swung open.

"Rob. Is something wrong with Terri? Is she sick?"

"No. She's fine. I need to talk to you." He gestured to the porch steps.

"I think you'd better come in. I've already dressed

for bed." She was wearing a pale green robe and gown made of nylon that clung to her body.

Rob, with his mind on their conversation, hadn't noticed her clothing until she drew his attention to it. He almost wished he hadn't come for their discussion. "Uh, you want to change clothes?"

"I'm wearing a robe," she said. "Unless it makes you uncomfortable."

Uncomfortable? Hell, it made him downright hot, but he could stand it. He had to, because he had to set things straight and then get out of here.

"Are you coming in?" she finally asked, and he realized he'd been standing there staring at her for several minutes.

"Yeah."

"Shall I put on a pot of coffee?"

"No. This won't take long."

She led the way into the kitchen, and his gaze remained fixed on her rear as it shifted beneath the nylon. Sweat broke out across his forehead.

"Iced tea?" she asked as he entered the kitchen behind her.

"Yeah, that'd be great." Something to get rid of his cotton mouth. To shake him from the sexual fantasies that kept popping into his mind as he watched her move.

She got them both glasses of tea and came to sit down at the table. Rob took a seat across from her, sipping the cold drink.

"It's warm tonight."

"You came at this time of the night to discuss the weather?" She grinned at him, knowing she was teasing him.

"Of course not."

"Well?"

"I'm here to discuss our engagement." Now let her see if she wanted to tease him.

"Oh."

When she said nothing else, his frustration rose. "That's all you've got to say? 'Oh'?"

"No. I can explain."

"I think I might like to hear that explanation."

She nibbled on her bottom lip and he wanted to put his mouth over hers, to stroke her full lips, to taste her sweetness, to—

"Rob?" she called, drawing his attention.

"What? Yes. You were going to explain."

"It's about the children."

With a sigh, he said, "I figured."

"Why would you realize that?"

"Floyd told me a lady overheard you telling the Social Services guy at the Prine ranch."

"I should've told you at once what I'd done. Did you tell Floyd we weren't engaged?" She leaned toward him, displaying a shadowy vee at the neckline of her gown and robe.

"No."

"Oh, thank you, Rob. I can't tell you—well, you see, Mr. Graham was going to split the children up…like they intended to do to me and my sisters when our parents were killed. I couldn't stand it."

"I can understand that, Melissa, but—"

"I know. But Mr. Graham is an old lady!"

Rob cocked one eyebrow. "Is that why they call him Mister?"

She doubled her fists and glared at him. "You

know what I mean. He's a prissy old man about a hundred years behind the times.''

''In what way?''

''He didn't think I should take care of boys without a man in the house. He was going to put them in three different homes. Can you believe it? Susie is only six. Wayne tries to be responsible for both Susie and Billy. He'd go crazy not knowing how they were doing.''

''That'd be bad,'' he agreed. In fact, he thought it would be criminal when the man had Melissa as an option. ''But you could run into trouble without a man in the house.''

''Don't you dare agree with that man!''

''I'm not agreeing,'' he hastily assured her, trying to hide his grin. Her green eyes were sparking and her cheeks were flushed. He'd never seen her look more beautiful.

''You managed to raise a girl all by yourself,'' she pointed out.

''But I needed you to help her when we went shopping.''

''But that's—anyway, I told Mr. Graham I was engaged so he'd think there was a man in the picture. Then…then he asked the name of my fiancé and…and your name came out of my mouth.''

''No local guy hanging around your doorstep?'' He'd wondered about that. After all, Melissa was beautiful…and rich. Those two items were always in demand.

She shook her head. ''No. They aren't interested in helping children.''

''Ready-made families aren't easy to deal with.''

She studied him, and he braced himself for whatever she said next. He never knew what to expect.

"Is that why you never remarried?"

He frowned. "That doesn't have anything to do with what's happened here."

"You asked about my personal life," she pointed out.

He glared at her, but she just waited for an answer. Finally he said, "Let's just say my experience with marriage wasn't the happiest time of my life. I couldn't think of any reason to repeat it."

"You let one bad experience put you off marriage completely?"

"Yeah." Hell, she had no idea how bad a marriage could be. He didn't ever want to give anyone that much control over him again.

"Well, look, you know the engagement's not real, but would you mind letting it stand for a little while?" She gave him a beautiful smile.

He shook his head, bringing alarm to her face. "No! I mean, I wasn't shaking my head no."

"Yes, you were."

"But I didn't mean to. I—never mind." He couldn't tell her that he was thinking her smile was enough to convince almost any man to do whatever she wanted. "I don't mind, I guess, but what if the kids hear about it?"

"I'm sure they won't. You know how it is in the country. Everyone talks about something for a day or two, and then they move on to the next scandal."

"Floyd knew about it."

"But the kids won't be talking to Floyd. The Prine kids aren't anxious to see anyone right now. And

Terri hasn't left the ranch except to go shopping with me. We all skipped church yesterday. At least, I assume you didn't go.''

"No. I told Terri we'd wait until you could go.'' It had been a relief not to have to face all those people in church. He needed time to settle in, too.

"So, you see? It really won't matter at all. Our being engaged will be old news in a couple of days.''

"How long do we pretend?'' he asked.

"I figure in a month or two, I'll tell Mr. Graham that we had a fight and broke up. By then, he'll see how well the children have adjusted and agree to leave them here.''

Rob thought her plan sounded overly optimistic, but he wasn't going to rain on her parade. Not tonight at least. "So all I have to do is keep my mouth shut?''

"That's right. It will be simple.''

She leaned forward again, and he fought the urge to take her shoulders and push her back in the chair, so he wouldn't be tempted to touch her. But then he'd be touching her. And he feared he might lose control.

"Uh, yeah.'' He stood. "Okay. I'll keep quiet.''

She stood, too, and moved toward him. "Oh, Rob, thank you so much.''

He reversed his direction and went the other way around the table. She gave him a surprised look but said nothing. He rushed through the kitchen door and headed for the porch. Some fresh air…and some distance…would help.

Following him to the door, Melissa caught his arm just as he'd almost made his escape.

"I wanted to thank you again."

He groaned. Now she'd done it.

"Rob? Are you all right?"

"Damn it, no, I'm not all right," he muttered, staring down at her. Didn't she have any sense at all? She should be backing away from him, not holding him close.

"What is it? Can I help?"

Frustration had built until it insisted on release. With a grim stare, he said, "Yeah, you can help. I think I deserve a reward for cooperating. And you're the one who can give it to me."

"What do you want as a reward?" she asked, frowning at him.

"This." He swept her against him, feeling her breasts against his chest, her small waist as his hands spanned it, and his lips covered hers for the kiss he'd been wanting since he first saw her.

It was as if time stood still. His body lit up, coming to attention. The frustration disappeared, replaced by a raging hunger to hold her closer, to taste her more. He was surprised when she didn't protest or pull away.

Even when he lifted his mouth from hers, she remained in his arms. He slanted his mouth over hers again and ran his hands over the silky material and the curvaceous body underneath.

When his jeans tightened to the point of discomfort, he realized he'd have to stop what was happening, or take it to another level. And he couldn't do that.

He broke off the kiss and put her away from him. She stared at him as if she was in shock. She probably was. He reckoned he'd come out of left field as far as she was concerned. She didn't seem to know much about men.

"I apologize. But don't invite a man in when you're dressed like that."

Then he made his escape into the night air and almost ran to his house. He considered running around it several times, to try to quiet his body, but he figured everyone would think he was crazy.

Instead, he went to the barn, pacing among the animals, trying to tell himself that nothing had changed.

Melissa was in shock.

She stared out into the darkness, but Rob had quickly disappeared. She was grateful he'd called a halt to what had happened, because she wasn't sure she would've remembered why it was a bad idea.

Frowning, she tried to remember now. But it was difficult. The children. That was it. When she'd told anyone her idea of a home for children, they'd told her she was crazy. The men she'd met would be glad to take her to bed. They'd be glad to help her spend her money. But they didn't want anything to do with someone else's children.

And she would not let anyone get in the way of her dream.

Now she'd found a man who liked children.

But he didn't want a wife.

And he probably didn't want a houseful of someone else's children.

In spite of that, he was an all-star kisser. Melissa had never been kissed like that before. She'd never lost track of what was happening. She'd never wished to give herself to a man.

Rob Hanson had changed all that.

And she was engaged to him.

That thought brought forth a shaky chuckle. A sham engagement. She'd have to keep her distance if she was going to remember that fact.

Lordy, lordy, he sure felt good, though.

After putting away their glasses of tea, barely touched, she trudged up the stairs, wondering how she'd ever get to sleep when her body was still humming from Rob's touch.

Good thing they were keeping the engagement a secret. That way he wouldn't have any excuse to touch her. And if he didn't touch her, she might be able to keep her lack of control a secret.

Rob had forgotten to ask Melissa about whether Abby knew about their pretense. So, the next morning, he pulled her aside as they all mounted up.

"Abby, I don't know if you heard, but…but Melissa and I are pretending to be engaged."

She gave him a relieved smile. "She explained? I'm glad. I was afraid you'd hear about it and…and be mad."

"No, I'm not mad. Floyd told me, but I told him we weren't making any announcement yet. But I thought you should know."

"It really is important for her, Rob. She has such a soft heart. She couldn't bear the thought of those kids being split up."

"I know. I just wanted to clear things with you."

Abby gave him a big smile. "No problem. I'm

happy to have you as my almost brother-in-law.''
Then she swung up into the saddle and rode after the
crew.

Rob stood there, staring after her. He wouldn't
mind being her brother-in-law. He had a lot of respect for Abby. He respected Melissa, too, but, most
of all, he wanted her. With every ounce of his body.
He hadn't gotten a lot of sleep last night.

He mounted his horse and rode after the others.
Hard work would be good for him. By the time he
got home tonight, he'd be so tired, he'd fall asleep
at once. No dreams. No cravings. No Melissa. That's
how it had to be.

He didn't ride back in until almost dark. Unsad-
dling his horse and giving him a good rubdown
didn't take all that long. He spent his time concen-
trating on the thought of supper.

He was starving, and he hurried to the house, eager
to see Terri and hear his requisite *Melissa said*s for
the day. He could allow himself that much, hearing
about Melissa. He just didn't want to see her.

Because then he'd want her too badly.

He was almost to the porch when he noticed a
piece of paper on the screen door. There were also
no lights on in the house. He ran up the steps and
grabbed the paper. He could just barely make out the
writing.

Come to my house. We have to talk.

                                    Melissa

Uh-oh. He figured his engagement was about to
end. She'd decided his mauling tactics from the night

before disqualified him from the marriage stakes.

Well, good enough. He didn't need this kind of torture. Instead of heading for Melissa's at once, however, he decided to take a quick shower and change clothes. No point in smelling like a horse when he got his walking papers.

Of course, she could want to discuss something about Terri, but Rob didn't think so. All day he'd been waiting for the ax to fall. He'd overstepped the line last night.

Fifteen minutes later, he came back outside and began a leisurely stroll to the brightly lit house. It looked as if every light in the house was on. She must have some whopping electricity bill.

But then, she could afford it.

He stood outside, breathing deeply, getting up the nerve to knock on the door.

Before he could, the front door popped open and Terri stood there beaming at him.

"Dad! Come on in. We've saved you dinner."

"Thanks, baby. Why am I eating here? Is there a problem?"

"Oh, Dad, you big tease!"

She grabbed his hand as he reached the door and tugged him in the house. "I can't believe you didn't tell me."

"Tell you what?"

"Melissa said not to say," a deeper voice said from behind Terri.

Terri flushed, but she kept smiling. "Dad, this is Wayne Prine. And Billy. Melissa's upstairs putting the girls to bed."

"I see. Well, it's good to meet you, Wayne, Billy," Rob said, nodding at the two boys. He was worried about what Terri had said, but he figured things would be explained shortly. "You said something about dinner?"

"Yeah, it's all ready. I know you're starving. We've already eaten. You worked extra late today."

"Yeah. Lots to do."

All three kids followed him as he headed for the kitchen. If he was lucky, he could finish eating and leave before Melissa came back down.

Ten minutes later his luck was still holding. He'd risen to carry his plate to the sink after a great meal when they all heard footsteps coming down the stairs.

"Uh, I gotta go," he muttered.

But it was too late.

Melissa came through the kitchen door. When she saw him, she came to an abrupt halt. Then she launched herself at him, wrapping her arms around his neck and giving him a kiss that rivaled his from the night before.

Chapter Six

Melissa pushed back from Rob's embrace before she forgot they had an audience. But it was difficult.

"Uh, Rob, sweetheart, the kids know."

His dazed look, as he lowered his lips to hers again, didn't indicate he understood her message.

"Uh-huh," he muttered and brought her back to him.

After another intoxicating kiss, she pushed away again. "Rob, the kids."

He looked at them, then back at her. "The kids."

Terri giggled. "You remember us, don't you, Dad?"

"Yeah, sure," he agreed with a frown.

It was an encouraging sign. Melissa pinched his waist on his side opposite from the children. "They know about our engagement. It's not a secret anymore."

He stared at her, and she saw dawning horror in

his eyes. It was time to get rid of the audience. "Kids, I bought a new movie yesterday. Why don't you go start it, and you can finish it tomorrow."

"I think you might be more fun to watch," Terri said, giggling again.

Fortunately, Wayne thought otherwise. "Come on, Terri, leave them alone. Let's go watch the movie." He grabbed his brother's arm and dragged him from the room. After a moment's hesitation, Terri followed.

Melissa let out a sigh of relief when the door closed behind them. Then she faced Rob again.

"I'm sorry."

"What happened? You said they wouldn't know."

She got a glass of water and moved to the table. When she sat down, Rob did, also. "I didn't know Mr. Graham would make a surprise visit today. I've only had the kids four days."

"He didn't expect me to be here, did he? I mean, I work. No self-respecting man would be hanging around the house all day."

"No," she responded, shaking her head. "But I had to introduce him to Terri, and...and he asked her how she felt about us getting married."

Rob groaned and covered his face with his hands. Big hands, hardened by work, but tender when he touched her. Her cheeks flamed and she looked away.

He took his hands down. "What did Terri say?"

Melissa licked her dry lips. She felt badly about what had happened, but she couldn't have avoided the revelation once Mr. Graham arrived. "I told him we hadn't told the children yet. Terri got all excited and...and she wanted to find you at once."

Rob shuddered at the thought. He could stonewall Floyd okay, but Terri? His daughter? "Thanks for avoiding that," he said, hoping she didn't hear the sarcasm he couldn't hold back. But she did.

Her shoulders hunched defensively. "I didn't intend—I didn't know what else to do."

"Yeah."

He could've yelled at her. Some men got angry when a woman involved them in something they didn't want, but he was being reasonable. Which, of course, didn't mean he would continue to be.

"Rob, I hope you're not upset."

"No, I understand. But it means we'll have to tell the kids the truth, and probably Mr. Graham, too. We can't pretend we're getting married when we're not."

She stared at her hands clenched together on the table and said nothing.

"Right?" Rob prodded.

"I can't do that!" Her voice was barely above a whisper, but her tone was vehement. "He'll take the children away! He made that clear today."

"Maybe if I talk to him—"

"No! Once he knows we're not going to marry, I will lose them." She didn't fight the tears that filled her eyes and spilled down onto her cheeks.

"Damn it, what am I supposed to do? Marry you?" he demanded, anger in his voice.

After tension-filled silence, she asked in a small voice, "Would that be so terrible?"

Rob felt as though he were trapped on a wild ride at the county fair ever since Melissa had come into the kitchen. Now, he simply stared at her, wondering if she'd lost her mind.

Terrible? It would be heaven. And hell. Marry the woman he lusted after? Marry the woman he admired? Marry someone who would have complete control over him because he couldn't deny her anything?

Fear ran through his veins. He'd thought he loved his wife. But that love had died swiftly enough. The emotion Melissa evoked in him, not love, he quickly assured himself, was powerful. And would grow the more he was around her.

"You're being ridiculous."

She looked as if he'd insulted her.

"Melissa, you deserve more than—you deserve a real marriage."

Her chin lifted and she dropped her gaze from his. "That's not an option. I want to care for these children. All it would be is a piece of paper. I'll pay all the fees."

"You think I'm saying no because of some piddling charge for a license?" he demanded, rising to his feet, unable to sit still for this bizarre conversation.

"No! No, I don't think that. But—look, I know it will be an inconvenience, but—"

"An inconvenience? To lie to my daughter, to marry you, when I never intended—" He came to an abrupt halt. The wrong words had bubbled to the surface. He didn't love Melissa, he affirmed to himself. He was attracted to her, yes, he'd admitted that days ago. But he didn't love her.

Anyway, she was talking about marriage as though

it were a trip to the grocery store. Didn't she understand it would change all of them forever?

"Couldn't we pretend for a little longer? Do we have to tell everyone today?"

Rob frowned at her. Time to burst her bubble. "Do you really think Mr. Graham will settle for anything less than a marriage? If he's here four days after you got the kids, do you think it will be his last visit? Do you think he will conveniently forget his prejudices because you give him one of your killer smiles?"

Tears rolled down her pale cheeks. He watched helplessly. What could he do? How could he promise to act out a lie that would endanger his...his heart. But how could he let her suffer like that? Or the kids.

He walked around the table and pulled her to her feet, wrapping his arms around her. "Don't cry, Melissa."

"I can't help it. What's so terrible about wanting to help children who have been hurt already? Why can't I do the one thing I have a talent for? I love making a good home. I love taking care of children. I—"

She buried her face against his neck and sobbed.

He couldn't take any more. She asked good questions. She was trying to do the right thing. She just needed a little help. Okay, so he might never recover from being in close proximity to Melissa. But those kids would have a chance to heal.

He kissed the top of her head, drawing in her scent, the smell of summer flowers, and muttered, "Okay."

"You don't understand, Rob. I—" She broke off

her protest to lift her gaze and stare at him. "Okay? Okay, what?"

"We can pretend we're engaged."

"But Mr. Graham won't be patient. He'd come every week because he has doubts about us getting married. I—I told him on Saturday that we were getting married next month, but I don't think he believes me."

He pushed her face into his chest again, because if he continued to look at her, he'd kiss her, he'd lose control. "I know. I'm agreeing to whatever you think is necessary."

"You'll m-marry me—for the children?"

"Yeah."

A look of incredible happiness came over her features. Rob prayed that he always made her happy. He couldn't bear to see her cry.

"Oh, Rob, you're wonderful!"

"Yeah." Like any man wouldn't agree to whatever she wanted. Panic built up in him again as he thought about what he'd done. And how it would affect his beloved daughter. He fiercely promised himself he'd protect his daughter's heart as closely as he would his own. Hoping to define his challenge, he asked, "Are we going to sign an agreement? I mean, how long will we…is there a time limit?"

That excited look disappeared and she stepped away from him. "Of course. We can sign whatever you want." She suddenly sounded stiff and formal.

"Hell, not for me!" he returned, letting out his frustrations. "You're the one with the millions. I mean, I have some money, but nothing compared to you."

She stepped closer again and reached up a soft hand to touch his cheek. "You were trying to protect me?"

"Somebody has to," he muttered, catching her hand and holding it against his face. He loved the feel of her.

Her sunny smile returned. "I don't think we need to sign anything. I'm sure you wouldn't take advantage of me."

"Damn! You're such an innocent! Look, you talk to Abby. Explain what we're doing. She'll tell you why you need to protect yourself."

"I'll talk to her," Melissa assured him, still smiling.

The growing need to taste her again told Rob it was time to head home. "I've got to get to bed. I have an early start in the morning."

"Okay. Rob...thank you so much for understanding."

"Yeah," he said, wondering if she understood that she was going to drive him crazy in no time.

First thing the next morning, Melissa called the main house. "Ellen, I need to talk to Abby. Does she have time to run by before she starts work this morning?"

"I'll ask her," Ellen assured her.

Instead of Ellen's voice, Abby's was the next she heard. "Everything all right?"

"Sort of. I need to talk to you, though. Have you got time?"

Abby was her big sister, sometimes bossy, but always there for her. She wasn't surprised when Abby promised to be there soon.

But she *was* surprised when someone knocked on her door as she hung up the phone. Abby wasn't that fast. She hurried to discover her younger sister on the doorstep. "Beth! You're back."

"Yes, we got in last night," Beth said, stepping inside to hug Melissa. "And I hear a lot has happened since I've been gone."

"What have you heard?" She didn't want to tell more than was necessary.

"I heard Abby hired a foreman?"

That was an easy question. "Yes, she did. Rob Hanson. I think he's met Jed."

"Met him? You mean, he knows him?"

"I'm not sure exactly. Rob certainly knew who he was, but he said he'd met him." She wasn't surprised when Beth pulled out a cellular phone.

"Let's ask him," Beth said.

"Come on in the kitchen while you're calling. I've got a pot of coffee on." She'd had to get up early to catch Abby before she rode out.

Beth followed her into the kitchen, murmuring into the phone. Then she said to Melissa, "Where's he from?"

"Somewhere in south Texas. I don't know the town."

Beth repeated the information into the phone. After she completed the call, she said, "Jed thinks he remembers him. If it's the man he's thinking about, he and his father had a spread in south Texas. He and Jed are about the same age and Rob wanted to follow the rodeo circuit, but his father was against it.''

"Could be him. He's about Jed's age." Something in her voice must've given Melissa away, because Beth stepped closer, staring at her.

"Is he good-looking?"

She licked her lips. "What does that have to do with anything?"

"I don't know. Depends on what you're thinking." Beth grinned. "But you sounded a lot like me when I had a thing for Jed."

"Had?" Melissa teased in return, hoping to distract her sister. "The last time I saw the two of you together, you couldn't keep your hands off him."

"My point exactly. Is it that way with you?"

"No! Of course not. But something else has changed. I'm now the mother of five children."

Beth knew how much the foster program meant to Melissa. She gave her another hug and began asking a dozen questions about the children.

Before Melissa could answer all of them, Abby walked into the kitchen.

"Beth! I didn't know you'd gotten back."

After they covered the details of Beth and Jed's trip, Abby turned to Melissa. All three were now sitting at the table, cups of coffee in front of them. "What did you need to talk about?"

It wasn't that Melissa intended to keep secrets from her sisters. She'd been prepared to ask Abby's advice. But now she'd have to try to explain herself in front of Beth, too. She took a drink of coffee and cleared her throat.

"Okay, here's the deal. Rob and I— Mr. Graham paid a surprise visit yesterday."

Abby frowned. "Can he do that?"

"He can do whatever he wants," she replied bitterly.

"What's the problem?" Beth asked, leaning forward.

"He doesn't think I should have boys in the house unless I'm married."

"But why did he let you have them in the first place, if that's the way he thinks?" Beth asked.

Melissa exchanged a look with Abby. With a sigh, she admitted, "Because I told him I was engaged and about to be married."

"You what?"

Beth's startled response brought a chuckle from Abby. "I felt the same way. Steady, responsible Melissa telling a big fat lie."

"Fortunately, you didn't react so obviously." Melissa felt awful for having to admit her lie. But she was glad it worked.

"Wait a minute," Beth said, her eyes narrowing. "You started out saying you and Rob. What does he have to do with any of this?" Then she answered her own question. "You said you were engaged to *him?* But he's been here less than two weeks. Melissa!"

"I know, but…but I'd spent the day with him at the mall and he was so good with Jessica and Mary Ann and—when Mr. Graham asked the name of my fiancé, his name came out."

Beth stared at her, a look of fascination on her face, as if she found Melissa's explanation amazing.

Abby, however, had questions. "I already knew all that. What did you need to discuss with me?"

Here came the hard part. "Rob agreed to marry me."

Both Abby and Beth leaped to their feet.

"Are you out of your mind?" Beth demanded.

"Melissa, you can't be serious?" Abby added.

Melissa didn't get up. She didn't look at her sisters. She sat quietly, composing herself. "He's a good man, and he's willing to marry me so I can keep the kids." Then she looked up. "I'm going to marry him."

Her sisters stared at her, letting her words sink in. Then Abby, with a nod, sank back into her chair and said, "What do you need us to do?"

It was Abby's calm acceptance that almost broke her control. As always, her sisters were her best friends. She reached out and squeezed Abby's hand. Beth grabbed her other hand, linking the three of them.

Rob pushed himself hard that day. It was the only way to escape his thoughts. The only way to control the panic that filled him.

He was riding fence in the afternoon. Not a pleasant task, but usually one he didn't mind. Today, he would've preferred any job but that one. It gave him too much time to think.

Terri, at breakfast, had chattered nonstop. She left him in no doubt of her approval. Which was a good thing, he guessed, until the marriage ended. He didn't know how long it would last, but when it ended, his job would probably end, also.

Oh, Abby wouldn't fire him. She was fair. But how could he stay? How could he see Melissa and yet not be able to touch her?

He shook himself. He was being ridiculous. Their marriage wouldn't involve touching. It was a paper marriage only. He had to remember that. Those kisses they'd exchanged, for the purpose of deceiving the children, couldn't happen again.

Abby found him around five. He intended to put in several more hours, to punish himself, if nothing else, but she ordered him back home.

"It's too early," he protested.

"I appreciate your dedication, but we're all having dinner together this evening to celebrate Beth and Jed's return."

"So you want me to cover some of your jobs so you can get ready? Sure, tell me what I need to do."

"No, Rob. I want you to have time to clean up before dinner. We're eating at Melissa's at six-thirty."

"Everyone's coming?" he asked, surprised. Abby was quite friendly with her hands, but he hadn't expected them to be treated as family.

"No, just family."

He processed the information and came to the realization that Abby knew about the marriage. "She told you."

"Yes."

"Abby, I tried to talk her out of it."

"I know, Rob. Don't worry about it."

"Did you tell her to have me sign a prenup?" He had to make sure Melissa had discussed that subject with Abby.

"No. She explained that you're doing her a favor. She said it would be an insult to do so."

"Hell, Abby, talk some sense into the woman!"

Abby laughed. "Melissa makes her own decisions, Rob. You try talking some sense into her. Be there at six-thirty, or we'll come looking for you."

After Abby rode off, he considered ignoring the invitation. But with Melissa's stubborn determination, he knew Abby hadn't been kidding about them coming after him.

Besides, he didn't want Melissa to cry again. He turned toward home, deciding maybe he should clean up a little early to see if he could do as Abby advised.

Talk some sense into Melissa.

An hour later, his hair still wet from his shower, dressed in a pair of pressed jeans and a dress shirt, he headed for Melissa's house.

Wayne opened the door to his knock. "Come on in. Melissa's in the kitchen."

"Thanks. Are the kids...I mean, where is everyone else?"

"Terri's helping fix dinner and I'm watching the brats," the boy said, then realized he'd used unacceptable terminology. "I mean, the little ones."

Rob smiled. "Good for you."

He waited until Wayne had disappeared into the large den where he heard the music from a Disney movie before he headed for the kitchen.

He passed the dining room and discovered it set with china and crystal. Should he have worn a suit? Apparently this was a formal occasion.

As he entered the kitchen, he was frowning, trying

to decide if he was inappropriately dressed. Terri and Melissa both greeted him, and he nodded.

"Dad!" Terri protested. "That's not how you greet your fiancée." She stepped over and pushed him toward Melissa.

Rob didn't know what to do. He knew what his daughter expected, but he didn't know what Melissa wanted.

As if she realized his dilemma, Melissa stepped toward him, her arms extended. With that kind of invitation, how could he keep to his earlier promises?

He pulled her against him and satisfied his daughter's expectations, satisfied Melissa's invitation, and, most of all, he satisfied the cravings he'd been fighting all day.

Chapter Seven

Melissa wasn't sure how long she was in Rob's arms. Not long enough. But then, forever would be too short. Terri's greeting to someone broke them apart.

She swallowed, her gaze still on Rob, devouring him with her eyes. What was wrong with her? The marriage was a paper one. She'd promised that before he'd agreed.

It was what he wanted.

"I guess you don't need any help in the kitchen," Beth said with a chuckle.

Melissa stepped over and hugged Beth and then Jed, who was standing behind her. "Um, no, everything's under control."

Except my libido.

"Jed, let me introduce Rob Hanson and his daughter Terri to you. Rob, this is Jed Davis, my brother-in-law. Oh, you haven't met Beth, either."

Though his cheeks were still flushed, Rob stepped forward and shook hands with Jed and nodded to Beth.

"Actually, I think we've met," Jed said, a lazy smile on his face. He smiled a lot these days. "But when I met you, this young lady wasn't around."

Rob pulled Terri into his arms. "Nope. But she's the best thing I ever produced."

"Dad!" Terri protested, but she was grinning.

The men exchanged friendly smiles.

"I've followed your career," Rob said. "You've certainly been successful."

"Thanks. Weird that we'd wind up at the same place, isn't it? How's your dad?"

Melissa intervened before Rob could answer. "Terri, fix both guys a glass of iced tea so they can sit on the patio and visit. If you go on out, Terri will bring it to you."

Rob gave her a strange look, but the two men left the kitchen. As soon as they were out the door, she took down a bowl and filled it with chips, then added a bowl of salsa, placing them both on a tray. "Can you put the tea on the tray and carry all of it, Terri?"

"Sure."

"Good. I suspect the men are hungry. Maybe this will keep them satisfied until dinner."

Terri left the kitchen, leaving Beth and Melissa alone.

"I'd say Rob's already satisfied, from what I saw."

"Beth!"

"Well, he looked like a happy camper to me. I thought you said this was a marriage on paper?"

"It is, but Terri…she thinks it's real. She pushed him to me and…it happened."

"Can you hire her on a retainer?"

"Beth, stop it!" Melissa complained, her cheeks red again. She was going to have to give up wearing blush if things didn't change.

"Everything all right in here?" Abby asked from the kitchen door.

"Abby, yes, come in," Melissa said with gratitude. "Beth was just teasing me."

"That's because when I got here, she and the handsome Rob were lip-locked and the heat was rising."

Abby sauntered over and took a chip out of the bag Melissa hadn't put away. "Well, you should know about steam, Beth. I think you drove poor Jed crazy for a while."

Melissa enjoyed Beth's red cheeks. She was glad it was someone else's turn to be embarrassed. Besides, she and Rob were keeping up appearances. That was all.

Which didn't explain the wish that everyone would go away and leave the two of them alone again. "Hormones," she muttered.

"Exactly," Abby agreed.

Melissa looked up in shock. She hadn't realized she'd spoken aloud. When she realized Abby thought she was talking about Beth, she breathed a sigh of relief.

"Hey, don't be too critical. All three of us have hormones," Beth assured them. "It's about time you started looking around, too, Abby. You can't keep focusing on cows all the time."

"If I'm going to turn a profit this year, I'd better. The market is all over the place."

Melissa breathed a sigh of relief as the conversation turned to ranch matters. No more personal questions. She could think about cows without any problems. She couldn't say the same about Rob.

Rob enjoyed his time on the patio with Jed. They had a lot in common. In fact, when Jed was explaining his need for some broncs for training purposes, Rob immediately thought of several horses he'd discovered in the Circle K herd that he thought would be well suited.

After questioning him, Jed was pleased. The conversation then turned to good rodeo stock, which sparked an idea in Jed's head. He made a mental note to talk to Abby about it.

"Dinner's ready," Abby announced from the door.

They both stood and followed her into the house. With eleven people at the table, six of them children, they didn't need a guide to find the dining room. The noise would've made it easy for anyone to find it. Melissa was telling the children where to sit. Rob caught her gaze and lifted an eyebrow, waiting for her direction.

The smile she returned rocked him. Its sweetness made him hungry for her, a hunger he was determined to deny. Then she gestured to the head of the table, the traditional place for the father.

He froze. The significance of his seat overcame him. What was he doing? How could he face these people? How could he—but they knew the truth. The adults all knew.

Abby, still standing beside him, took his arm and started him in the direction he needed to go, as if she understood his panic. Which bothered him even more.

Then he saw the smiles on all the faces. Terri was watching him with pride. Jed sent him a look of sympathy as he took his place next to him, beside his wife. The other children seemed okay with him sitting there, too. Wayne was on his left hand, across from Jed. Rob decided Melissa had deliberately divided the table, putting all the males at one end.

Jed leaned forward. "Does this mean we can talk about horses all the time? No discussions of fashions, or recipes or babies?"

Beth elbowed him in the ribs.

"Oops, sorry, sweetheart," he said, but he was laughing.

Wayne joined in the laughter, then a guilty look crossed his face.

Rob patted him on the shoulder and said under his breath. "It's all right, son. They'd understand."

He wasn't sure his words would reassure the boy, but he hoped they did. He knew when his mother died, he'd felt guilty for days whenever he smiled. How could he do so when she was dead? He knew, from things Terri had said, that the Prine children were adapting, but there had been some rough moments when Susie had cried or the boys had bogged down in their grief.

Wayne gave him an abrupt nod.

Here's a HOT offer for you!

Get set for a sizzling summer read...

with 2 FREE ROMANCE BOOKS and a FREE MYSTERY GIFT!

NO CATCH! NO OBLIGATION TO BUY!

Simply complete and return this card and you'll get **2 FREE BOOKS** and **A FREE GIFT** – yours to keep!

Visit us online at
www.eHarlequin.com

- The first shipment is yours to keep, **absolutely free!**
- Enjoy the convenience of Silhouette Romance® books delivered right to your door, before they're available in stores!
- Take advantage of special low pricing for **Reader Service Members only!**
- After receiving your free books we hope you'll want to remain a subscriber. But the choice is always yours—to continue or cancel, any time at all! So why not take us up on this fabulous invitation, with no risk of any kind. You'll be glad you did!

315 SDL C4FD

215 SDL C4FC
(S-R-OS-07/00)

▼ DETACH HERE AND MAIL CARD TODAY! ▼

Name:	
(Please Print)	
Address:	Apt.#:
City:	
State/Prov.:	Zip/Postal Code:

The Silhouette Reader Service™ —Here's how it works:

Accepting your 2 free books and gift places you under no obligation to buy anything. You may keep the books and gift and return the shipping statement marked "cancel." If you do not cancel, about a month later we'll send you 6 additional novels and bill you just $2.90 each in the U.S., or $3.25 each in Canada, plus 25¢ delivery per book and applicable taxes if any.* That's the complete price and — compared to cover prices of $3.50 each in the U.S. and $3.99 each in Canada — it's quite a bargain! You may cancel at any time, but if you choose to continue, every month we'll send you 6 more books, which you may either purchase at the discount price or return to us and cancel your subscription.

*Terms and prices subject to change without notice. Sales tax applicable in N.Y. Canadian residents will be charged applicable provincial taxes and GST.

If offer card is missing write to: Silhouette Reader Service, 3010 Walden Ave., P.O. Box 1867, Buffalo, NY 14240-1867

BUSINESS REPLY MAIL
FIRST-CLASS MAIL   PERMIT NO. 717   BUFFALO, NY

POSTAGE WILL BE PAID BY ADDRESSEE

SILHOUETTE READER SERVICE
3010 WALDEN AVE
PO BOX 1867
BUFFALO NY 14240-9952

NO POSTAGE
NECESSARY
IF MAILED
IN THE
UNITED STATES

From the other end of the table, Melissa said, "Rob, would you ask the blessing?"

She hadn't given him warning, and Abby, seated beside her, leaned forward as if to intervene, but he nodded and bowed his head. Before he could begin, however, Melissa spoke again.

"Could we all join hands? It makes it seem more like family."

Rob reached out for Jed's and Wayne's hands, figuring it was the first time he'd held hands with other men. Maybe he'd discuss the seating arrangements with Melissa next time. He'd much rather be holding hands with her.

After a quiet blessing, a buzz of conversation filled the room as the dishes were passed around the table. The three women helped the children around them fill their plates. Terri helped, too. She was seated between Jessica and Mary Ann.

Rob realized his daughter had never looked happier. The past few years she'd seemed a little withdrawn. But since she'd been taken into Melissa's "family," she'd been happy.

With surprise, he realized he'd been happier, too, in spite of the frustration and diverse reactions he had to the beautiful woman at the other end of the table.

He stared at Melissa. When she turned and caught his gaze, she again gave him that smile, the one that turned his insides to mush and made him want to haul her up the stairs to the nearest bed.

Not a good idea.

And after you're married? an insidious little voice

inside him asked. Not that kind of marriage, he reminded himself again.

"Say, Abby," Jed said, speaking to her over the heads of the kids, "Rob says you've got a couple of horses that might be good for training my bronc riders. Interested in selling them?"

Abby looked from Jed to Rob, then back again. "We do?"

Rob assured her they did.

"Probably," Abby said, smiling at both men. "We'll talk after dinner."

Jed nodded, satisfied.

Again Rob thought of his earlier idea. He knew there was a booming business in providing bulls for the rodeo. But his interest was in horses. He wondered if Abby would be interested in diversifying into raising and training broncs for the rodeo. He planned on getting on Terri's computer that night and seeing how much information he could find.

When they reached dessert, the ladies cleared the dirty dishes from the table and retreated to the kitchen. In a couple of minutes they returned with saucers and a huge chocolate cake.

Beth came back to her seat next to Jed, but she didn't sit down. "Before we serve the cake, Jed and I have an announcement to make."

She tugged on his arm and he stood beside her, wrapping both arms around her. Even Melissa looked surprised.

"An announcement? What is it?"

Beth looked at her husband with eyes full of love, and Rob had to look away so jealousy wouldn't fill him.

"We're going to have a baby," Beth said, her voice singing with happiness.

Noise erupted around the table. Both Melissa and Abby ran to hug first Beth and then Jed. Though the pair had only married last fall, about eight months ago, everyone was happy. It took several minutes before they calmed down. Then Melissa began serving the cake.

"Does that mean we have to leave?" Jessica asked softly, her voice wobbly.

Melissa put down the knife and sat down again. "Jessica, why would you ask that?"

"'Cause that's why Mommy and Daddy left us. Daddy said he didn't have room for another damn kid unless he got rid of us. And he did."

The tragedy of her words pierced Rob's heart. But he didn't have to worry about reassuring the little girl. He was coming to know Melissa well. She knelt beside Jessica's chair and wrapped her arms around first her and then Mary Ann.

"No, angel, that's not what it means. Beth has her own house. Besides, we have plenty of room. There'll always be a place for you here. For both of you."

Beth smiled. "It means you'll kind of have a cousin. Have you ever had a cousin before?"

The little girls shook their heads no.

"Well, it's almost like having a sister or a brother, only they live in another house. You'll like it."

"Hey!" Terri suddenly said, a big grin on her face. "I will, too. Have a cousin, I mean. 'Cause when Dad marries Melissa, you'll be my aunt."

"That's right," Beth agreed. "And I'll have a ready-made baby-sitter."

Smiles were shared around the table, except for Rob. Not that he wasn't happy for Beth and Jed. He was. A baby was a wondrous event. He wouldn't mind having more children. But that required a wife. A real wife.

He stared at Melissa. When he'd agreed to the marriage, everything had seemed black and white. A simple response to a simple problem. But every day, it grew more complicated. And his daughter was part of the complication.

Maybe he should insist on a prenup, after all. One that required their marriage to last ten years. Then Terri would be twenty-two, out of college. Able to understand how these things happened when they got a divorce.

Then maybe she could explain it to him.

The next day, Rob thought a lot about the pretense he and Melissa were involved in. He finally decided, as he was riding in that night, that they should tell Wayne and Terri the truth.

They were old enough to understand what was happening, and Wayne, at least, had a vested interest in keeping their secret. He was pretty sure Terri could be trusted, too.

After taking care of his horse, he trudged over to the manager's house, noting with a sigh that it had no lights burning. Was he expected to go to Melissa's every night?

There was no note this time, but there also was no food. The thought of one of Melissa's hot meals was enough to draw him to Melissa's house even if he didn't have anything to discuss with her. It was after eight by the time he'd showered. He figured if he ran across anything not moving on the way, he'd snatch it up and start eating.

He revised his plans, however, when he found Wayne sitting on the front porch steps, all alone, his head buried in his arms.

Without saying anything, Rob sat down beside the boy.

The wrenching sobs pouring out of the boy subsided when he realized he wasn't alone. He hastily wiped his red eyes and muttered, "I got something in my eyes." But he didn't look at Rob.

Rob stared straight ahead. "Yeah. That happened to me a lot when my mom died, too."

Wayne sniffed. "Bet you were younger, though."

"A little, but it doesn't much matter what age you are. When it's someone you love, it's hard."

"Yeah."

"Anything in particular set you off?"

There was a long silence, and Rob wasn't sure the boy would answer.

Finally he said, "It's silly."

Rob waited.

"Susie called Melissa 'Mama.'"

After a moment Rob said, "She's pretty little."

"I know. But next thing you know, Billy'll be calling you 'Daddy' and they won't—" Another sob escaped the boy.

"Remember their parents? Sure, they will. It's just the way little kids cope." After a moment he added, "Just like crying. It helps ease the hurt."

He guessed he hadn't figured out what was wrong, because Wayne didn't respond. Then it hit him. "You're worried they won't need you anymore? Is that it?"

Wayne looked away from Rob. "I know it's selfish, but I've done my best. I can't—"

Rob put an arm around Wayne. "Son, you've done an incredible job of being there for your brother and sister. Terri's told me about you hugging them when they cry. You've tried to be both parents. No one can do that good a job. But they'll always need you. You're their big brother." Rob paused and then added, "If they find someone else to sort of be their parents, it means you can go back to being what you are. A really special big brother."

"I don't want to let Mom and Dad down," Wayne said in strangled tones.

"Never in a million years. They're up there in heaven right now bragging to all the other angels about you, boy."

Wayne bowed his head for several minutes. Then he looked at Rob. "You think so?" His voice was wobbly, as was his smile, but Rob was relieved.

"I know so. Because if you were my son, I'd be busting my buttons with pride."

Several tears ran down the boy's face, but his smile grew stronger. "Thanks, Mr. Hanson."

"Let's make it Rob. We're going to be family, so there's no need to be formal."

"Do you think we'll get to stay here?" Wayne asked, and Rob could hear the anxiety in his voice.

"I think Melissa will fight like a mama bear if anyone even thinks of taking you away."

Wayne gave a watery chuckle. "Yeah, she can be fierce, can't she?"

"Yeah." They sat together for several minutes, Rob's arm still resting on Wayne's shoulders. Then his stomach growled. "Sorry, Wayne. I'm kind of hungry."

"You'd better go in. Melissa saved you dinner. And it was real good."

"You coming?" Rob asked as he stood.

"Um, I'd better wait a few minutes."

Rob studied the silent boy. "Say, I think I forgot to lock the tack room door. Would you mind going to the barn to check on it for me? I'm tuckered out and starving or I'd—"

Wayne was already on his feet before Rob finished. "I'd be glad to. I wanted to ask about helping out, but I didn't know—"

"You worked on your dad's place?"

"Yeah, and I'm worried about that, too."

"When you get back from the barn, we'll talk about some chores around here for you. And we'll talk to Melissa about what they're going to do about your place."

Wayne's shoulders squared and he smiled again, more confident this time. "Thanks, Rob. I'll be back in a few minutes."

Rob watched the boy stride toward the barn. The tack room door was locked, but the boy needed something to do, a purpose. Rob felt badly that he hadn't thought of that before. His mind had been on Melissa and their pretend engagement. But Wayne's life had been turned upside down. It was work that would make him feel right again.

He turned and knocked on the front door. Terri opened it to him.

"We've been worried about you," she said, but she was on tiptoes trying to peer past her father.

"Really?" he asked dryly, but she didn't even notice.

"Yeah, it's late. You're usually home before now."

He stood there and watched his daughter. Finally he said, "And you're checking to see if someone followed me home?"

"Oh! No, but Wayne was— I mean, I thought he was out here. He seemed upset earlier and—" She broke off and shrugged. "I was worried about him."

He considered teasing her again, but he didn't have the heart. "He's okay. He's gone to the barn to do an errand for me."

"Oh. Well, come on in."

Instead of waiting for her father, she hurried ahead of him to the kitchen and Rob could hear her telling Melissa about Wayne's whereabouts.

When he entered the kitchen, Melissa was taking a covered plate out of the oven.

"You must be starving. What do you want to drink?" she asked with a smile that lit up his insides.

"Iced water would be good."

"Okay, and I'll make a pot of decaf for later." Melissa looked at Terri, standing by the table, and said, "Terri said you asked Wayne to run an errand for you. Nothing's wrong, is it?"

"I thought I might've left the tack room unlocked, and Wayne volunteered to go check it for me. Nice kid."

"Yes, he is. Terri, why don't you see if Billy wants some company until Wayne returns? I think he may be lonely."

As Rob knew would happen, Terri immediately agreed to Melissa's suggestion and left the kitchen.

"The little girls already in bed?"

"Yes. They played outside a lot today, and the sunshine wears a child out. Was Wayne really all right?" She came to the table and sat down across from him, her eyes anxious.

"He's fine. But we need to talk about some chores for him."

She straightened in her chair. "No, of course not. Not yet. He's too…it's too soon after his parents' deaths."

"It's almost been a week, Melissa," he said softly. "The boy needs to feel useful. He needs to believe that life goes on."

"Is that why—" She stopped, staring at him. "Oh, dear, I didn't understand. Maybe Mr. Graham was right. Maybe I have no business taking care of boys. I should've realized that." She jumped up from her chair and began pacing the room, wringing her hands. "I didn't know what to do when he exploded then ran out of the house. I decided I should wait, let him come back on his own, but I've been scared to death and—"

Rob couldn't stand it any longer. He stood and pulled her against him the next time she passed by, wrapping his arms around her.

Stroking her hair, he whispered, "Shh, Melissa, stop saying things like that. You did the right thing. Everything's all right. They're going to be fine."

Her body trembled against him and erotic thoughts filled him, thoughts of stroking every inch of her, removing her jeans and shirt so he could touch her. He was a snake to think about that when she needed comfort.

Or maybe he was just a man.

"Oh, Rob, I was so frightened," she said, burying her face in his chest. "I thought all I needed was love to do this job, but…it wasn't enough tonight."

"Most parents have situations they don't know how to handle, Melissa. And love is about the best guide you can have. Somehow, things work out."

"But I don't even know what upset him. How can I avoid it next time?"

"I doubt if you can avoid it, but I can tell you what happened."

She backed out of his hold. "You can? You talked to him?"

"Yeah, I talked to him. Susie called you mama tonight."

"Well, yes, but she did it accidentally. I don't see how—"

"Wayne's been trying to be mother and father to Susie and Billy. He felt like he'd let his parents down when Susie turned to you."

She teared up again, and Rob hugged her.

"Now, don't cry again. You know how susceptible I am to tears," he teased. "You can ask me to do anything if you're crying, and I can't resist."

His exaggeration—at least, he hoped she thought it was an exaggeration—brought a watery chuckle for a response. He kissed her temple, then gave a dramatic sigh. "I don't mean to be a complainer, but do you think I could eat my dinner before break-fasttime?"

Chapter Eight

Melissa watched Rob the next morning. She'd insisted he come to her house for breakfast as a reward for the way he'd handled Wayne. And the late hour he'd gone home. He showed no signs of the emotional ordeal of last night. He was as easygoing and friendly with the children this morning as he'd always been.

But not only had he consoled Wayne last evening, before he got his supper, he'd also sat in on a long discussion at her kitchen table with her and Abby and Wayne. He'd been supportive and innovative when talking about his ideas for dealing with Wayne's family ranch. Today, he was taking Wayne over to the Prine ranch.

He was back to being perfect again.

"Why can't I go, too?" Billy asked, drawing everyone's attention.

"Because it's going to be a long day and not much

fun," Rob said, smiling at the child. "Besides, with me and Wayne going over to your place, we need someone here to keep an eye on the girls."

"Hey!" Terri protested.

Melissa raised an eyebrow. "I'm with Terri. We manage just fine."

Rob leaned toward Billy, his voice taking on a confidential air. "They always say that until a bug appears."

"Bugs are fun!" Billy protested, frowning at his sister and her new friends.

"And that's exactly why you need to hang around. Girls don't think like us."

"You can say that again," Melissa whispered as she passed by Rob on her way to the sink.

He grinned at her, making him look all the more handsome. Then he turned his attention back to Billy. "We'll plan a day when we all go back to your place. But Wayne and I have a lot to do today."

Melissa noted the look of purpose on Wayne's face. It made him look older...and satisfied. Unlike the past few days. Rob had been right in what Wayne needed. He'd said men needed to be doing something. And now he was giving Billy some purpose. Killing bugs for the girls.

"When will Miss Abby talk to the lawyer?" Wayne asked.

Rob looked at Melissa, waiting for her to answer.

"She said she'd call him this morning. But she'll have our lawyer draw up the corporation papers." Last night, Rob had suggested they form a corporation, the Circle K and the Prine estate, that would provide rodeo stock. They could use the Prine ranch land and pay half the market value for rental into the children's trust. They would maintain the ranch land, keeping its value high, until the children were adults and could make their own decisions about the land.

Abby had been in agreement, but she'd insisted it be a three-way partnership, with Rob being the third partner. When Wayne had agreed, Rob had reluctantly accepted their offer. After all, he would provide the experience and knowledge necessary. He felt he could operate the business and still give a lot of time to the Circle K.

He'd discussed whether Jed should be a partner, but Abby, after calling her brother-in-law, said he'd offer advice and any connections he had with the rodeos, but he had too much to do as it was. He couldn't take on more work right now.

So, in the space of one evening, Rob had solved several problems.

Melissa had been lucky when she'd claimed Rob as her fiancé, even if she hadn't known it at the time.

"You ready, Wayne? We told Duffy we'd be there by eight," Rob reminded him.

The boy pushed back from the table and carried his dishes to the sink. "Let me go grab my hat."

"Dad," Terri said, though her gaze was following Wayne's exit.

"Yeah?"

"I came up with a name for your company." She'd sat in on the discussions the evening before, though she'd kept quiet.

Melissa stared at Terri. She'd worried that Terri felt left out, but the child was so well balanced, she had handled everything well. "What did you think of?'' she asked, intrigued. They'd debated several names the night before, but nothing had seemed right.

''It's really pretty simple, so you may not like it,'' she said, watching her father.

He nodded, indicating she should go ahead with her idea.

''ProRide.'' She paused, looking at both adults. ''With the *P* and the *R* capitalized, but all one word.''

Melissa immediately replied, ''I like that.''

''Me, too,'' Rob said, smiling. ''Good job, Terri.''

Wayne came back into the kitchen.

''What did Terri do?'' he asked.

''She came up with a name for our corporation,'' Rob said, explaining.

Melissa noted Terri's shy look at Wayne. The girl wanted his approval even more than her father's. She crossed her fingers for Terri.

''Hey, that's great,'' Wayne agreed. ''I like it being short. Do you think Abby will like it?''

''I think she'll love it,'' Melissa assured them all. And Abby would, because Melissa would tell her how important it was to Terri. ''After you two have gone, we'll call and tell her before she talks to the lawyers.''

''Which is our signal to get out of here,'' Rob said, rising to carry his own plate to the sink.

Melissa took it from him before he could.

He muttered thanks. Then, to her surprise, he bent down and brushed her lips with his. ''See you later,'' he called to everyone, and was out the door before Melissa could even think of anything to say.

Okay, so he wasn't perfect in one respect. His goodbye kisses were way too short.

She looked at all the children still sitting at the table and decided, considering their audience, he might even be perfect in saying goodbye, too.

But she didn't have to like it.

Rob still wasn't sure he should be a part of the corporation, but he was excited about the prospect. It was going to involve a lot of work, but it was work he liked. He could even put some of his savings into it. But when he'd offered last night, Abby had told him that wasn't necessary.

"I won't have time or expertise to deal with it, Rob. And while Wayne has some expertise, when school starts, his involvement will be limited. The brunt of the work will fall on your shoulders. That's your part of the investment."

Even with his mind on last night, Rob still recognized the tension that filled the boy beside him when they turned onto his family property.

Casually, Rob said, "Your dad was a good manager. Looks like the place is in good shape."

"Yeah," Wayne agreed, clearing his throat. "He worked hard."

"I imagine we'll need to hire several hands to help with everything here and on the Circle K. Did your dad plant hay, to prepare for winter?"

"We've got two big fields," Wayne assured him. "Last time I looked, they were doing well."

"We can treat the hay like the land rental, pay half the market value, with the money going into the trust."

Wayne gave a sigh, the tension easing. "Rob, I was worried about providing for the three of us. You make everything easy."

Rob's heart ached for the boy trying to do a man's job. But he wasn't going to tell Wayne that. Grinning, he teased, "You won't think so in a few days. You're going to work your tail off, boy. You'll be glad when school starts, so you can rest."

"That'll be a first," Wayne said. "I don't always do so good in English."

"Hey, be nice to Terri, then. She aces that class. She'll tutor you."

Wayne shot him a look, but by then they had arrived at the ranch house. It was time to get down to work.

When they got back to Melissa's that evening for dinner, Rob was well satisfied. He and Wayne had talked to Duffy, the old cowboy who was taking care of everything on the Prine ranch. They'd evaluated the stock. They'd even repaired fence when they found some damage.

A sense of accomplishment filled him. They'd made a lot of progress and he was excited about their new venture. He knew Wayne was much happier. Everything was perfect.

Except for his engagement.

In the back of his mind, he'd reconsidered his idea that Terri and Wayne could be told the truth. After last night, he knew the boy beside him, while doing his best to be an adult, was still a child. As was Terri.

His daughter was terrific. She was an excellent student, a hard worker. And happy. But there had been something missing from her life. A woman's touch. She had bonded with Melissa so quickly, the need, one he hadn't recognized before, was obvious.

Which only made everything so much more complicated.

Rob stopped the truck at Melissa's door to let Wayne out.

"You're not coming in?" the boy asked.

"I'll be back in a few minutes. I want to check on a couple of horses in the barn. Then I'll clean up."

"Need any help?"

Rob appreciated the offer. He knew Wayne was tired. The emotional toll of returning to his home for the first time since his parents' deaths would've been enough, but the boy had worked hard as well. "Thanks, but I can handle it. Your job is to reassure your brother and sister. I imagine they're waiting to hear everything is okay."

"Yeah," Wayne agreed with a sigh. "Thanks again," he added before getting out of the truck.

Alone at last, Rob let his mind wander to the real problem. Melissa. Not that there was anything wrong with Melissa. No, but his feelings for Melissa, feelings that were strengthening every minute he spent with her, were inappropriate.

And he didn't know what to do about them.

Maybe they could stretch out the engagement, give him some time to work things out, figure out how to deal with her.

Yeah, that was the ticket. He'd talk to her tonight about stalling Mr. Graham. Surely, between the two of them, they could come up with a way to do that.

* * *

"You're sure he said he'd be right back?" Melissa asked Wayne again. She'd fed the younger children earlier. When Wayne came in, Terri had volunteered to eat her dinner with him.

"That way you and Dad can have a quiet dinner together," the young girl had added, winking at Melissa.

She would've protested that idea, should have protested that idea, except that the events of the day made private conversation absolutely necessary.

Because, without consulting her fiancé, she'd managed to set a wedding date.

Catching a glimpse of a strong, handsome cowboy out the kitchen window, striding toward her house, she hurried to the front door, pulling it open before he had time to knock on it.

"Well, good evening," he said with a smile. A wary smile, with tiredness a part of it.

"Good evening." She stood still, waiting for him to make the first move, but when he didn't, she returned the kiss he'd given her that morning. A brief one, shorter than she wanted it to be.

"Wayne said you had a good day," she added as she moved back, her voice breathless. She sounded like an infatuated teenager, she decided in disgust.

He cleared his throat. "Yeah."

"Hungry? I made meat loaf."

The sound of running feet stopped him and he looked up the stairs to see three little girls heading his way, followed by Billy.

"I killed all the bugs," Billy informed him, his little chest swelling with importance.

"Good man." Rob praised him with a smile.

"We were good," Jessica said, a hopeful look on her face that made Melissa's heart ache.

Rob squatted down, putting his eyes on the little girls' levels. "I bet you were. I was, too. Do I get a hug for being good?"

All three little girls threw themselves at him. Amid their squeals, he wrapped his arm around all of them and stood to spin in a circle. Then he lowered them to the floor again.

Mary Ann, still silent, beamed at him and reached up to pat his cheek. The two older girls were giggling. Billy, his eyes wide, was standing to one side.

Rob stood and curled his finger at the boy. "I don't discriminate," he told him.

"What does that mean?" Billy asked as he stepped to Rob's side.

"It means you get a hug, too." He swept the boy up for a bear hug, then set him down again.

Melissa blinked back tears. How had he known? She guessed she didn't give him enough credit. She'd realized how left out Billy was feeling, but she hadn't expected Rob to do so. Obviously she was underestimating him.

"Again, again!" Susie cried, reaching up her arms. Instantly the other two girls joined in, even Mary Ann voicing her wants.

Rob repeated all the hugs, but Melissa knew he must be tired. And hungry. And he still had to hear her news.

"Okay, that's enough. When you're tucked into bed, maybe Rob will come tell you all good-night. Everyone head upstairs. I'll be right up to run your bathwater."

Billy, Jessica and Susie started up the stairs. Mary Ann, however, lingered, her little hand tugging on Rob's jeans.

"Yeah, sweetheart?" he asked, squatting down again.

She put her thin little arms around his neck and whispered, "I wuv you." Then she ran for the stairs.

Rob appeared embarrassed, his cheeks red, but Melissa was thrilled. "Rob, that was wonderful."

"What?" he asked, frowning at her.

"Mary Ann doesn't speak very often. And both she and Jessica are scared of men. But you've won their hearts."

He shrugged off her compliment. "Kids are easy to love."

A surprising protest rose in her. She wanted to insist she was easy to love, too. But Rob had already told her he didn't want her love. And she didn't love him, did she?

"Come on. I'll put your dinner on the table, then go bathe the kids. Terri and Wayne are eating, so you'll have company."

When she'd done all that, she hurried up the stairs, glad to postpone what she had to tell him. She wasn't sure he'd be pleased.

Rob took his time over the delicious meal. It was a good thing he worked hard, or he'd start putting on weight. Wayne's appetite matched his, however, so he didn't feel so bad.

For the first time since he'd met the Prine children, Wayne was talking like a kid, discussing school with Terri. He'd been worried about the crush his daughter seemed to have on Wayne. The best cure to a crush was to get to know the person better. Warts and all.

He grimaced. He didn't think Melissa had any warts.

"What is it, Dad? Did something taste bad?" Terri asked. She'd put a plate of oatmeal raisin cookies on the table to finish off their meal.

"No, baby—I mean, Terri. These are great cookies. Did you make them?"

"We all did," she said with a big smile. "It was a lot of fun. Jessica and Mary Ann had never made cookies before, but Susie, Billy and I had. We got to show them what to do. Only Mary Ann kept eating the dough. Melissa was afraid she'd get sick."

"You're not getting tired of the work?"

"Nope. Melissa paid me today. I'm ready to go shopping again." Her teasing smile told him she knew what his reaction would be.

Not wanting to disappoint her, he gave a shudder of distaste. "No, thank you."

"Oh, Dad, you had a good time, and you know it."

"I've had worse times," he grudgingly conceded. "By the way, Wayne, you'll draw a salary this summer for the work you'll be doing. But all three of you will receive some kind of allowance from the trust."

"Are you going to draw a salary?" the boy asked, watching Rob suspiciously. He didn't want any preferential treatment.

Rob grinned. He liked this kid a lot. "I already draw a salary, but I'm planning on increasing it some for the extra work. I'll need to if this young lady takes many more shopping trips.''

''Dad!'' Terri protested, but she was grinning.

The two males exchanged a superior look, then lapsed into chuckles.

Melissa entered the kitchen. ''Well, you three seem to be having fun.''

Rob let his gaze rove over her trim figure. Her hair was mussed, curling around her face, and there were several damp spots on her shirt, testifying to the nightly bath ritual. But he thought she'd never looked more beautiful.

When her gaze met his, he quickly shifted his to the cookie in his hand. ''A man ought to have fun when he's got cookies like these. They're great.''

''So, the way to your heart is with cookies?'' she teased in return.

How could he answer that? She already had his heart, even when she didn't want it. ''Yeah, sure,'' he said, taking a bite to preclude any more conversation.

''The kids are waiting for you to say good-night, if you don't mind. You could finish your cookies later.''

''Okay,'' he agreed. Anything to put some distance between them.

When he came back down the stairs a few minutes later, he returned to the kitchen to find only Melissa waiting for him. ''Where are Terri and Wayne?''

''They're watching a show on television, though I'm not sure Wayne will be able to stay awake until it's over. He must've worked hard today.''

''He did. Plus, it was tough on him going back to

the place for the first time. But he managed just fine.''

''I'm sure you helped. I was impressed last night, the way you worked everything out. It's going to ensure the kids' futures. And hopefully make you some money.''

''It will. I had another idea today.''

He frowned when she seemed distracted, scarcely acknowledging his words. ''Melissa?''

''Oh, yes, what was it?''

''I thought we could enclose the yard around the Prine house and rent it out. The rent could go into the trust fund, and the renters would help keep the place in good shape. It will fall apart if it stands empty.''

''That's a good idea. We'll have to get approval from the kids and the lawyer in charge of the estate, but I don't think that will be a problem.''

''Unless the kids want to move back over there with a guardian.'' He threw out that idea, knowing Melissa wouldn't like it. But it might solve a few problems.

''No!''

He had her full attention now. ''I wasn't saying it was a good idea, but it is an option.''

''I don't think that will work. Susie and Billy need—need mothering. They're too young.''

Rob nodded. He hadn't thought his idea would be acceptable to her. He picked up another cookie.

''Um, Fourth of July is coming up.''

At that non sequitur, Rob stared at Melissa. ''Yeah?''

"It's a big holiday here. Lots of people have parties."

"Okay." Was she wanting to have a party? Did she expect him to object?

"Everyone takes off work." She got up from the table and moved to the sink, with her back to him.

"What's going on?" he finally asked.

She spun around. "Nothing! Well, almost—nothing. Mr. Graham came back today."

"And?"

"He was pleased that Wayne was with you."

"Good."

She was twisting her fingers together and he knew that meant trouble. What had the man insisted on now? He remembered his intention to ask Melissa about stalling the wedding. Maybe—

"I told him we're getting married on July the fourth," she said with a rush, her chin lifted in the air.

Chapter Nine

So much for his plan of extending their engagement. The Fourth of July fell on a Monday. Less than two weeks away.

"I know I should've talked to you first, but he was pressing me for a wedding date," she said in a rush. "It seemed like a good idea at the time."

"Sweetheart, are you sure you want to do this? You've only known me a couple of weeks."

"Are you backing out?" she asked, alarm on her face.

"No, but…even if we pretend to care about each other, all your friends are going to think you're crazy." And they would be right.

Her bottom lip was trembling and Rob feared she was going to cry again. He couldn't bear that. He stood and moved closer, running his hands up and down her arms.

"You've changed your mind, haven't you?" she whispered.

"No! That's not what I meant. But there are problems. Things we didn't think about."

"Like what?"

Her fast comeback left him unprepared. He gathered his thoughts. "Like how long we're going to pretend. And how we'll explain everything to Terri…and the other children."

She pulled away from him and crossed to the window, staring out into the gathering dusk, folding her arms over her chest.

"You want a time limit?"

He followed her, unable to stay away. Settling his hands on her shoulders, he eased her body back against his. "I'm trying to be practical, Melissa. Someday you'll want a real marriage, your own children. I can accept that, but I want to protect Terri."

She spun around to stare at him. "Protect her from what?"

"From heartbreak. She already worships you. How will she feel when she discovers it's all a sham? When she has to stop being a part of your family? When she loses another mother?"

Her gaze grew fierce, reminding him of his description to Wayne at the idea of anyone trying to take the children from her. "She'll never lose me! I love her. I'll always love her and she'll always be a part of my family."

He couldn't avoid the comparison between Melissa and his ex-wife. Terri's birth mother walked away from her without a backward glance. Melissa, who'd only known his child for three weeks, loved her and refused to even consider letting her go.

He stared into her eyes and knew he could make no more protests. If Melissa was willing to put her personal life on hold for the sake of the children, he would accept her decision. After all, he had no personal life to put on hold, except for Terri. And she would be in good hands.

"Okay."

"You always say that, like I'll understand exactly what you mean," she protested. "Okay what?"

"Okay, we'll have the wedding on July the fourth. Do we get to have fireworks?"

"Do you want them?" she asked, smiling at him.

The only fireworks he was interested in would occur in a bed. But that wasn't on the schedule. So he'd have to settle for the Fourth of July kind of fireworks. "Sure."

"Then we'll have fireworks."

He smiled but took several steps back from her. Melissa in a compliant mood was too hard to resist. "Okay, what do I need to do to prepare?"

"Have your suit cleaned—no! Let's have a cowboy wedding," she suggested. "It will be too hot to wear a suit outside."

"We're going to be married outside?"

"Well, the Fourth celebration usually is a big barbecue. We could have it here on the ranch with dancing afterwards. So if you wear a dress shirt and jeans, I'll find something casual to wear, and we'll both be comfortable."

"Are you sure you want to do it that way?" He swallowed. Had she suggested this kind of wedding because it wasn't a real one? Was she saving the white satin and the church for her next wedding? "I mean, most ladies like a more formal occasion."

"I think my way will be more fun. And all the children can be a part of it. Would you mind?"

"No, I won't mind." He backed up several more steps. Just thinking about Melissa as a bride was heating him up. He needed to keep his distance. "Well, I'd best head out. It's been a long day."

"You don't want to discuss any more details?"

There was a hint of disappointment on her face, but Rob had reached his limit. Not even for Melissa could he promise to maintain control of his cravings. "Nope. I'll leave the details to you. Just tell me if there's something I need to do." He'd managed to back his way to the kitchen door. With a nod, he turned and walked out, calling for Terri as he did so.

She came out of the den. "Yeah, Dad?"

"Time to go home, baby. You ready?"

"I guess," she agreed with a sigh. "Wayne's about to fall asleep, anyway."

The boy, who'd followed Terri from the den, protested, "Hey, I was just resting my eyes."

Terri looked at Melissa, who'd followed Rob out of the kitchen, and giggled. "Yeah, right."

Rob held out his hand and Terri slipped hers into it. He headed for the door.

"Wait!" his daughter protested.

"What? Did you forget something?"

"No, you did. You haven't kissed Melissa goodbye."

Rob's gaze flashed to Melissa's. Temptation personified. But he couldn't test himself tonight. "Uh, I took care of that in the kitchen."

Fortunately for him, Terri accepted his explanation. "Oh, okay. Good night, everyone."

And they escaped into the darkness.

Melissa began planning her wedding at once.

In spite of her sisters' earlier protests that she was moving too quickly, she knew they would offer their support. They at least understood her reasons.

The children, once Jessica and Mary Ann were reassured that the wedding wouldn't change their status, were excited. Terri, when Melissa asked her to be her maid of honor, was beside herself.

"Me? The maid of honor? Oh, Melissa, that would be wonderful! I mean, don't you want your sisters?"

"If we were doing a formal wedding, I would, but I think it will be more fun to have it outside and keep it informal. And you're part of my family, now. My oldest daughter."

She became alarmed when tears filled the young girl's eyes. "Terri, what's wrong?"

"I—I'm going to love having you for a mother. Can I call you 'Mom'?"

Melissa enveloped her in a hug even as she remembered Rob's warning. She squeezed tightly, promising herself to never let Terri go. To keep her safe and love her forever. "Of course you can," she whispered.

Terri pulled out of her arms, blinking rapidly to dispel the tears. "Everything's so great! Where am I going to sleep? Will I get to have my own room?"

"Of course you will," Melissa said automatically.

And she had plenty of bedrooms. The house had six of them. Right now, the two boys shared a room and the three little girls were in another one. Melissa thought Susie would be happier being with the other girls instead of being by herself. That left plenty of bedrooms.

"Why don't we go upstairs and let you pick out which room you want? You can have your choice of two." One bedroom was downstairs. The master was up, so she would be readily available should one of the children need her during the night.

Everyone but Wayne trouped up the stairs with them, eager to start the changes that were going to occur. Wayne had gone with Rob again.

Terri picked out her room, the one at the end of the hall that looked out over the barn area. Jessica caught her hand as they headed back for the kitchen. "Will you sleep here tonight? Will you tell us a bedtime story?"

Terri looked at Melissa. "I could sleep over if...if you wanted me to."

"I'd love to have you here, honey, but how would your father feel about it? It would leave him all alone." Melissa had sometimes sensed a loneliness in Rob.

"I'll ask him. Are they over at Wayne's place today?"

"No, I think they're looking at the Circle K's herd of horses today. They're coming in for lunch."

When Rob had picked up Wayne that morning, she'd asked if they wanted to come for lunch. Rob hadn't been enthusiastic, which hurt her feelings, but Wayne had accepted before he'd realized it wasn't what Rob wanted. The man had agreed, even though Wayne offered to eat a packed lunch.

Did he want to avoid her?

He'd certainly avoided kissing her last night. He'd outright lied to his daughter. And *she* hadn't gotten a good-night kiss. Maybe he wasn't as attracted to her as she was to him.

That was a terrible thought to have about someone she was going to marry. One of the reasons she thought the marriage would work is that she enjoyed being with Rob. His presence made the day brighter, the night cozier. Somehow, he intensified everything around him.

And he made the children happier.

She'd never found a man more interested in the children's happiness than his own. Until Rob. She'd known right away he was a good father because of Terri. But his gentleness with the others, the time he gave Wayne, his sensitivity to their needs, made him the perfect man for her plans.

But it might be a disaster if he didn't enjoy being with her.

She settled the children at the kitchen table with a coloring project and asked Terri to keep an eye on them. She had to call the Reverend Jessup and ask him to officiate at the wedding. She also had to call a bakery about a wedding cake, and the local florist about flowers. Then there was the—

A knock on the front door halted her lists. She discovered Beth waiting patiently.

"Come in. What are you doing?"

"Nothing. Jed's afraid for me to do anything since

we found out I'm pregnant. The only thing he wants me to do is interview housekeepers. I'm bored."

"Well, I'm about to end your boredom. I need help and you'll be perfect."

"Help with what?"

"Planning my wedding."

Beth studied her sister. "You've set a date?"

"July fourth."

"You're kidding? That's less than two weeks away!"

"I know. That's why I need help."

Beth hugged her, then stepped back. "Are you sure you're doing the right thing?"

Melissa turned away, unable to face her sister's penetrating gaze. "I have to do this. I can't let them take the Prine children away."

Beth's arm came around Melissa's shoulders again. "Have you told Abby?"

"I haven't had a chance. Rob and I just agreed on the date last night. Mr. Graham paid another of his visits yesterday."

"I wondered what had sped things up. I thought it might be that you can't keep your hands off the sexy Mr. Hanson." Beth grinned, but she watched Melissa carefully.

Even though her cheeks turned red at the implication, which, she knew, had more than a shred of truth, Melissa denied her sister's words. "Of course not. It was Mr. Graham. He kept pressing me for a wedding date, and...and the Fourth popped into my mind."

"Yeah, you always did like fireworks."

* * *

Rob had lots to think about as they worked with the herd of horses. Such as where he was going to sleep once the marriage took place. And how many cold showers a day would he have to take? Cold showers weren't so bad during the hot summer, but in the winter they were hell.

"What about that roan?" Wayne asked him.

"Hmm? Oh, yeah, you're right, he might be good. He's big and strong. Let's cut him out." They'd already picked out seven horses that exhibited signs of good rodeo stock. After lunch, he figured he'd try a few of them out.

"After we put him in the corral, we'd better break for lunch. We'll need to get cleaned up before we sit down to eat."

After they returned to the barn and cared for their mounts, Rob suggested the two of them wash up at his place.

"Who's going to live here after you marry Melissa?" Wayne asked.

Rob raised one eyebrow. "You thinking about asking for it?"

"Me? And give up Melissa's cooking?" the boy asked with a big grin. "Not on your life."

"Smart man," Rob agreed, grinning back. "Having someone do your laundry, the cooking and the cleaning is a real bonus. Don't ever forget to show your appreciation."

"I won't. Does Terri do all that for you?"

"No, we do it together, most of the time. The cooking, since we moved here, has been done by Melissa, for dinner. Ellen offers a packed lunch most days and I'm on my own for breakfast. I let Terri sleep in when I can.''

"But she helps Melissa a lot.''

"Yeah. Melissa is teaching her things I couldn't. I'm pleased about that.'' And he was. Terri would be better able to cope if she were taught the essentials of keeping house. No matter who she married.

He shook his head. It was ridiculous to think of his girl child marrying, but, in reality, in six years she'd be thinking of it herself.

After dousing his head under the faucet, which immediately cooled him off, Rob rubbed his head dry and combed his wet hair. Then he rolled up his sleeves and scrubbed his hands with soap.

Wayne did exactly as Rob did. He grinned. Terri had imitated him a lot as a little girl, but he'd never had a son to follow him around. He kind of liked it.

As they walked over to Melissa's house, Wayne asked, "When are you two getting married?''

It surprised Rob that everyone didn't know, but he realized he and Melissa had agreed on the Fourth only last night. "The Fourth. We're going to have a big barbecue here on the ranch and get married then.''

"Wow! That's only a few days away.''

"Yeah.''

"Hey, that'll be great. Do we get to come?''

"Of course you do.'' He started to ask the boy to stand up with him, be his best man, but he wasn't sure it was what Melissa would want. He'd better check with her first.

Wayne said softly, "It's almost like we're family.''

"What do you mean?"

The boy shrugged his shoulders. "You know, families have big celebrations, do things together. Being included in the wedding is like we're family."

Hell, he wasn't going to ask Melissa. "I'm glad you feel that way, 'cause I was wondering if you'd be my best man."

"Me? You want me to be your best man?" Wayne asked, his voice rising in excitement.

"Well, I don't know too many people around here. I've spent the most time with you, and I like you best, anyway," he assured him, a grin on his face.

"Hey, yeah! I'd like that—if Melissa doesn't mind."

"She won't. I get to choose my best man."

"What do I have to do?"

"Stand beside me. Keep the ring safe until it's time."

"What about a bachelor party?"

Rob grinned. The boy had a frown on his face, as if worrying about providing a stripper hiding in a cake. "I don't think we need one of those. I've already had one, and they don't add much to the party."

Wayne sighed with relief. "Good, 'cause I don't know anything about bachelor parties."

"Best keep it that way for a few more years."

They reached the porch and Rob started to knock on the door.

"We don't have to knock," Wayne protested. "I live here. Melissa said so." He grinned at Rob. "And you'll live here in a couple more weeks."

"Yeah, I guess you're right." Of course the boy

was right. But that didn't make Rob feel any easier about walking into Melissa's house without warning.

However, her alarm system was working perfectly. Terri and the other four children came running when they heard the door open, as if they'd been listening.

"Dad, guess what!" Terri called over the other children's voices.

"What, baby?"

"I'm going to be Melissa's maid of honor!" She beamed at him, as if she'd been named Miss America.

"Hey! I'm going to be Rob's best man!" Wayne announced right back at her, his smile huge.

"Oh! That's perfect!" Terri proclaimed.

Rob watched the two of them. He thought it might be a good idea to keep an eye on those two. They were at the age where hormones kicked in and reason flew out the window. He liked Wayne, but he didn't want him getting carried away with his daughter.

Melissa came into the hallway from the kitchen. "Ready for lunch?"

Terri ignored her words and repeated Wayne's announcement. "Isn't it wonderful?"

Rob watched her, wondering how she'd react. He should've known better.

"I think it is. I'm so pleased, Wayne." She stepped forward and kissed the boy on his cheek.

Wayne turned a bright red and stared at Melissa, Ah, Rob thought. Poor Terri. Her hero had a crush on Melissa. It relieved Rob's worries, but it brought its own concerns. Terri's heartbreak. Wayne's heartbreak. Teenage angst.

Rob chuckled. At least it gave him something to

focus on rather than his own feelings. He and Wayne were going to have a lot in common.

Before Rob and Wayne returned to work, Melissa offered to escort Rob through her house, so he could see where he would live.

The children all wanted to accompany them, but Melissa limited their escort to their own rooms. It was quiet time, when the younger ones napped and anyone too old for a nap read a book for an hour.

They headed for the bedrooms. The first was the one shared by the three little girls. The room had a huge king-size bed. All three girls had plenty of room. The youngest, Mary Ann, slept in the middle, content to be surrounded by her sister and new friend.

Then they went to Wayne and Billy's room. The younger boy opted to read, of course, since he considered himself much too told to have a nap. Melissa had found him some books on dinosaurs. When she offered them to him, he tried to act nonchalant, but he reached for them eagerly.

Wayne sat down beside his brother, offering to look at the books with him for a few minutes, asking Rob to call when he was ready to go back out.

"I don't see why I have to read if Wayne gets to go to work," Terri protested, after proudly showing her father her new room.

"I'd think you'd want to spend some time in here. You've never had a room this pretty," Rob said.

"It is great, isn't it? Dad, do I have to wait until the wedding to move in? I mean, I spend most of my time here, anyway. Why don't I go ahead and move in?''

Before Rob could answer, Melissa slipped her hand through his arm. ''Why don't you let your dad and I discuss it, Terri? We'll let you know our decision later.'' Rob had tensed. She didn't know if it was her touch or Terri's request that had brought on that reaction.

''Okay, but—''

''Terri, you heard Melissa,'' Rob said sternly.

Melissa smiled at Terri, hoping to tempt a smile in return. ''I'm going to show your dad the rest of the house. Do you have something to read? Because I picked up the new *Seventeen* magazine at the store if you want to read it.''

Terri immediately opted to read the magazine.

''Is that magazine good for her?'' Rob asked after they closed the bedroom door behind them. ''I mean, she's only twelve.''

''It's a good magazine for all teenagers. And it makes her feel all grown-up to read it.''

''Yeah,'' he agreed, but he didn't seem happy about it.

Melissa wasn't too happy, either. She realized the next room on the tour would be her bedroom. Their bedroom. The immensity of what she was doing suddenly hit home.

She was going to share a bedroom with the hunk beside her. But not a bed.

Chapter Ten

Rob was already uptight, but he felt Melissa join him in that state and wondered why. She wasn't upset about Terri growing up. She wasn't upset about touching him, or she wouldn't have done it.

So what was the problem?

He figured it out when she led him to the opposite end of the hall. Without saying anything, she opened a closed door and walked inside.

It was a large, spacious room, but all he saw was the big bed. He cleared his throat and got right to the point. "Nice room. Where am I going to sleep?"

She walked over to smooth a wrinkle out of the blue-and-green plaid comforter that covered the bed. With her back to him, she said, "We'll have to share this room so the children won't say anything to Mr. Graham that would make him question our marriage."

Share the room. Not the bed. Even the thought of

sharing this space with the beautiful woman across from him was enough to make Rob shake. He'd thought he could do this, marry for the sake of the children. Now he wasn't so sure.

She turned to face him. "It's a big bed."

He stared at her as if she'd lost her mind. And she must have, or she wouldn't make such a ridiculous suggestion.

"This won't work," he said abruptly, and walked out of the room.

She followed him all the way down the stairs. "Rob, wait."

He finally halted when he reached the entryway. Close to the door so he could make a quick escape.

"Rob, didn't you realize… I mean, the whole idea is to convince Mr. Graham that we're married."

"I don't see why we have to convince him of anything. Invite him to the wedding. He'd have proof that way. A piece of paper is all he needs. That's what you said." He glared at her, determined to win this argument.

"Rob, he can take the children away whether we're married or not if he thinks the home we're providing isn't—doesn't meet their needs." She moved closer, her face earnest as she tried to convince him.

All he could think about was pulling her against him and kissing her senseless. Until he persuaded her to *really* share her bed as well as the room.

"I can't do it."

"What? Share the room with me? I promise I'll give you your privacy, Rob. I mean, I'll get up before you and finish in the bathroom before you get up.

You usually shower before dinner. I'll shower before bedtime. Or in the morning. We'll work out a schedule."

A damn schedule. She thought everything could be solved with a schedule. She was too naive to be believed.

"I can't share a bed with you," he rasped, being as specific as he could. The thought of even being in the same room with her when she emerged from a shower, fresh, damp, her hair curling in tendrils around her beautiful face, her naked body wrapped in a towel, was making him hard.

He turned his back on her before she could see his reaction.

"But, Rob—" she began, and he felt her moving around to face him.

He bolted for the door. "Tell Wayne to meet me at the barn."

Melissa spent the rest of the day trying to think of how to handle this latest crisis. She supposed Rob could use the downstairs bedroom, but she knew the children would figure that out quickly. And even a casual comment from the children about their not sharing a bed would give Mr. Graham pause.

It wasn't until she was talking on the phone to Ellen late in the afternoon that she thought she'd found a solution. Ellen had been cleaning out the attic and had come across some old water floats she and her sisters had used one summer in the swimming hole that formed naturally in the creek.

"I've got to ask Abby if she wants to keep them,"

Ellen said with a sigh. "They make much better ones these days, and they're not very expensive."

"I'm sure she'll want to throw them away, Ellen," Melissa said, even as she planned to look in the catalogs she had to see what was available. If Rob wouldn't share the big bed, she could sleep on an air mattress in her closet. It was a walk-in.

"Oh, by the way, I heard today that you've set a wedding date. Have you told Abby?" Ellen asked.

"We didn't decide until last night. I was going to come tell her this evening. I didn't think word would spread that quickly." Melissa felt badly that Ellen had found out from the local gossips. "Would you mind not mentioning it to Abby until I can?"

"Of course I won't. But what have you planned?"

"It's going to be July fourth. I thought we'd have an outdoor wedding and a big barbecue afterwards, with dancing. I'm trying to arrange everything so it won't be a lot of work for you."

"Don't worry about that. Everyone will bring a dish, like we always do. A side of beef is easy to handle. Have you arranged for a wedding cake?"

"I called today. Tomorrow I'm going into Wichita Falls to make my final choice. I wondered if you could keep an eye on the children? Terri is going to go with me. We should only be gone a couple of hours."

"Of course I can."

"Ellen, you're so wonderful. It's almost like having a real mother," Melissa assured her. Since the woman had come to work for them when Melissa got sick last fall, she'd become a part of their extended family.

"You couldn't say anything that pleases me more, dear. You and your sisters are pretty wonderful, too."

Melissa hung up the phone, a weight lifted from her shoulders. At least she had a solution to offer Rob. She'd been dreading him coming home, afraid he would've decided to call off the wedding.

Maybe that would be best, she thought morosely, then straightened her shoulders. She couldn't betray Wayne, Billy and Susie, no matter what.

She'd hoped, she finally admitted, to convince Rob that being married wasn't so bad. That maybe they had a chance to make their marriage real. He was the perfect father. She wanted him to be the perfect husband, too.

Every time he touched her, shivers consumed her. When he'd held her close, those few times he'd kissed her, the shivers had turned into flames that almost consumed her. She'd been kissed before, but never the way Rob kissed her.

Did she love him?

She didn't know. She only knew that thoughts of him filled her. That every time he avoided touching her, pain shot through her. That when he did touch her, no matter how casual, she felt electrified.

Worst of all, when he was near, she almost forgot all about her need to care for the children.

She shook off those thoughts and began preparing dinner, dealing with the constant interruptions of the children, hoping the distraction would calm her nerves until she could talk to Rob again.

Rob wouldn't let Wayne try out any of the horses they'd selected. He knew Melissa would never forgive him if the boy got hurt. So he took the rides himself.

And got hurt.

He landed on his left shoulder. Though there was no real damage done, he had a bruise that was painful.

Wayne dropped off the corral fence and rushed to him. "Are you all right?"

Rob tried a smile, but he didn't think it was too successful. "I think it's just a bruise."

"Maybe you should see a doctor," Wayne suggested as Rob struggled awkwardly to his feet.

"Nope. I haven't broken anything. But I think we made a good choice with that horse. He's going to be a great one. He's got some incredible moves. Think you can catch him and remove his gear?"

He watched the boy corner the horse, then ease to his head. Wayne was great with horses. Even as young as he was, he did the work of a trained cowhand.

Once Wayne had taken care of the horse, Rob suggested they call it a day. "I think I'm going to need to rest my shoulder until tomorrow."

"I still think you should see a doctor," Wayne said, looking concerned.

Rob, with his good arm, clapped the boy on his shoulders. "Don't worry about me, Wayne. I'll be fine. I'll clean up before coming to the house."

Once Wayne was out of sight, Rob sighed. His shoulder hurt like hell. He hurried to his house, though every step pained him. As soon as he reached the kitchen, he dug out the aspirin. Then he headed for the shower. He stood under the hot stream of water until it began to cool.

After drying himself, he wrapped the towel around his waist and returned to the kitchen to seek out the bottle of liniment he'd used before when he'd had an ache or pain.

"Are you looking for this?"

He spun around, almost dislodging his towel, to discover Melissa sitting at the kitchen table, the bottle of liniment before her.

"What are you doing here?" he demanded, tightening the towel around him.

"I came to see if you're all right. Wayne said you hurt your shoulder." She stood and came toward him.

His breathing sped up and he backed away. "Uh, Melissa, I'm fine. I told Wayne I was fine."

"But you were looking for the liniment, weren't you?" She stepped closer still. "How will you rub it into your shoulder without help?"

"I'll manage," he muttered, his teeth gritted.

She straightened her shoulders and, using her sternest tone, ordered him to sit down. "*I* shall apply the lotion to your shoulder. And if you are not better in the morning, I shall drive you to the doctor."

Her care for him was so endearing, it almost unnerved him. And made him much too susceptible to her charm. "I can get Wayne to apply the stuff. It smells and you don't want to mess with it."

"Oh, please! When we first came to the ranch, we made daily applications of the stuff. We weren't used to riding every day." Melissa laughed even as she pushed Rob toward the nearest chair.

"Really, Melissa, you shouldn't—" He shouldn't have attempted to twist around to face her. The pain that shot through him made speech impossible.

"Oh, Rob, sit down at once." She helped his descent by pushing on his good shoulder. Then she began rubbing the liniment into his left shoulder, her hands warm and caressing.

He closed his eyes and indulged himself in a daydream of his loving wife caring for him. When he'd been young and in love, he'd envisioned that kind of life. He'd work hard all day and come home to a loving wife, a houseful of children, hot food and well-deserved rest.

Until reality struck.

And he'd been left with a baby to raise on his own.

"Does that feel better?"

Her soft voice awakened him from his thoughts.

"Yeah, much better. I'm sorry you had to bother but—"

"Don't be silly. You've done, are doing, so much for me and the children. I owe you more than I can ever repay."

Rob stood abruptly. "Yeah, thanks. I'll dress and be up to the house for supper."

She looked at him strangely, and he wondered if he'd made a mistake. "I am supposed to come up for supper, aren't I? Or are Terri and I eating here?"

"No, of course not. Dinner is waiting. You don't need any help dressing?"

He stared at her in surprise.

Her cheeks flamed and she added, "I mean, putting on your shirt."

"I'll manage." He edged his way out of the

kitchen before turning and hurrying to his bedroom. It would take a little longer than usual to dress, but not because of his shoulder. He'd have to wait until his jeans would fit properly. And he'd have to think about horses or cows or hay to bring that about.

Definitely not about Melissa's soft hands stroking his bare flesh.

When Melissa came out of Rob's house, she saw Abby heading her way. "Abby!"

"Hi. Were you checking on Rob? One of the hands saw him take a nasty fall. I thought I'd check on him."

"He's fine. I rubbed liniment into his shoulder. He thought it would smell too badly for me to touch it. Do you remember how much we used it when we first came here?"

Abby chuckled. "Yeah. Instead of perfume, we wore eau de liniment."

"I was going to come see you after dinner tonight," Melissa said, fearing Abby would return to her house.

"Oh? Is there a problem? I can come to you after dinner if it would make things easier. After all, I don't have a bunch of kids to keep an eye on."

"Why don't you join us for dinner? Then I won't feel so bad about making demands on you after a hard day's work. We can call Ellen from my house and tell her."

"Are you sure you have enough? You have quite an army to feed. Even more than when you were cooking for all the hands," Abby pointed out.

"I know. It's amazing how things have changed

in the last year. Aunt Beulah would be surprised if she could see us now.''

"Especially Beth. Married and pregnant. We're going to be aunts, Melissa. Isn't it amazing?''

"Yes, it's wonderful. I would be jealous if I didn't have my own family.'' But it wasn't her charges she was thinking of. A picture of Rob floated before her.

"You haven't forgotten that they're only temporarily with you, have you, Melissa? I worry about what would happen if Jessica and Mary Ann's parents came back for them. Or if Mr. Graham took the Prine kids away.''

"He won't have a reason to. That's what I wanted to talk to you about. We've set a date for the wedding.'' Melissa slanted a glance at her sister and then looked away. "It's July fourth. I thought we'd have a big barbecue and an outdoor wedding.''

Abby came to an abrupt halt, grabbing Melissa's arm, which forced her to stop, also. "Honey, do you know what you're doing? I mean, I like Rob. I think he's a good man, but you've only known him a few weeks. Don't you think you should wait?''

Melissa stubbornly shook her head. "No, we've got to settle matters now. We're agreed.'' Abby wasn't showing any signs of agreement and she tried again. "Please, Abby, this is what I want.''

With a sigh, Abby started walking again. "You know I want you to be happy.''

"I know. This marriage will make me happy. I couldn't face myself in the mirror if I let Wayne, Billy and Susie be torn apart, lose what little family they have left.''

They'd reached Melissa's front porch and Abby stopped again. "What do I need to do?"

"Oh, Abby, thank you," Melissa said, hugging her sister. "You and Beth are so wonderful."

"I don't know about that, particularly if you expect me to decorate a wedding cake or hand-print invitations. You know my handwriting is terrible."

Melissa beamed at her sister. "With computers, you don't have to worry about that. We're going to print up invitations and mail them out next week. I've already started making calls. Oh! I asked Terri to be my maid of honor. We're going to keep it simple and include the children. Wayne's going to be Rob's best man. You don't mind, do you?"

Abby hugged her again. "No. I think that's sweet. So you're going to be a mother before Beth is. I guess I'll be the old maid aunt who baby-sits for the two of you!"

"Don't be silly! The right man will come along for you, too, Abby. Then we'll all be happy together," Melissa assured her sister.

Arm in arm, they entered the house, where six hungry kids were waiting.

It was almost an hour after Melissa left him before Rob was prepared to go to dinner. The aspirin had dulled the ache in his shoulder, as well as the liniment Melissa had applied.

But he dreaded facing her. Not only because her touch was still fresh in his memory, but also because they hadn't resolved their sleeping arrangements. He didn't have an answer, but he knew he couldn't trust himself to share a bed with her and keep their marriage on paper only.

Terri answered his knock, swinging wide the door. "Are you okay, Dad? Wayne said you hurt your shoulder."

"Yeah, it's just a little stiff. It will be fine by morning."

Wayne came up behind Terri. "Did it turn black and blue?"

"It's working on it," he assured the boy with a lopsided grin.

The younger ones, having heard Wayne's question, stared at Rob.

"I want to see," Jessica said.

"Me, too!" Susie called.

Mary Ann stared at him but said nothing.

"I've had bruises," Billy bragged.

Before anyone could continue the discussion, Melissa came out of the kitchen. "Kids, go watch your video. Rob is tired and hungry. He needs to eat."

The children headed for the den. Terri, before she followed the others, reached up and kissed his cheek. "I'm glad you're okay, Dad."

"Thanks, baby," he said softly. It bothered him that her concern wasn't as sweet as Melissa's.

"Abby's here. We've both waited dinner on you," Melissa said when they were alone.

"You shouldn't have waited."

"I didn't realize it would take you so long to dress. I was about ready to come help you," she assured him, a smile on her lips that made him hungry for more than food.

He followed her into the kitchen, because he had

no choice, giving thanks for Abby's presence. It would destroy the sense of intimacy that overtook him whenever he and Melissa were alone.

"Hi, Rob. How's the shoulder?" Abby asked as she carried glasses of iced tea to the table.

"Fine. I'm sorry I held up dinner."

"No problem. Melissa has plenty of lists to keep us busy until you got here. There's so much to do to get ready for a wedding."

Rob's gaze flew to Melissa and he caught the look of apprehension she cast his way. Did she think he was going to back out? He'd given his word. He would marry her…but he wouldn't share her bed. Not that way.

"Uh, yeah. I guess there are." He couldn't think of any details that needed to be done. He'd asked Melissa last night, but she'd said for him to show up. It suddenly occurred to him that he'd need a ring for her.

"Uh, I may have a few things to do myself. Can I have a couple of hours off one of these days?" he asked. "I'm sorry to be taking so much time off, but after things settle down, I promise I won't—"

Abby chuckled. "Please, Rob, I know you're a hard worker. But you're going to be my brother-in-law and we're business partners in ProRide. Take whatever time you need. In fact, tomorrow might be a good day so you can rest your shoulder. It's bound to be sore."

Since it was still aching tonight, Rob knew Abby was right, though he hated to admit it.

"I think he should see a doctor in the morning, just to be sure he didn't do any real damage," Melissa said, putting a casserole dish on the table that filled the room with wonderful smells. "But so far, he refuses. He's a stubborn man."

"What man isn't?" Abby agreed.

"Wait a minute. When you consider what lengths Melissa is willing to go to keep the Prine kids, I don't think I'm the one who is stubborn."

He realized at once he'd embarrassed Melissa, but Abby seemed to accept his words.

"He has a point, Melissa. Could be ladies can be stubborn, too. Aunt Beulah certainly was. Remember that time she was determined to dig for water right outside the house?"

Melissa laughed, which chased away her embarrassment. "Well, she did find water."

"Yes, but that well is twice as deep as any well on the ranch, as the man assured her it would be."

"Yes, but if she hadn't been so stubborn, I'm not sure she would've taken on three little girls who needed her so badly," Melissa added.

"True," Abby agreed with an answering smile. She picked up her tea glass as Melissa sat down at the table with them. "Here's to stubbornness...and to your marriage. May the two of you be happy."

Chapter Eleven

When Abby left after dinner, Rob tried to accompany her back to the ranch house. Melissa wasn't letting him get away so easily.

"Oh, Rob, could you wait just a minute? There are a couple of questions I need to ask you."

He paused, frowning, while Abby, after another goodbye, headed for her house.

"Quit looking like you've been ambushed," Melissa muttered, irritated by his obvious reluctance to spend any time alone with her.

"It's been a long day," he replied, not looking at her.

His words reminded her of his injury, and she felt guilty. "Sit back down, so you can be comfortable."

"I'll stand. What questions?"

Stubborn man. She reached for the catalog she'd marked earlier in the day. "I have a solution to our...our bed problem."

After one glare, he looked away. "Yeah?"

Opening the catalog, she held it in front of him. "See? I'll buy an air mattress. I can put it in my closet and sleep there at night."

He stared at the picture in the catalog. Then he looked at her. "If anyone sleeps on an air mattress, it'll be me. It's your bed."

"But your closet isn't as big as mine and—"

"You heard me, Melissa," he growled.

She raised her eyebrows. "Do you think you're going to be giving the orders around here?"

He opened his mouth, as if ready to fire off an answer, then closed it again. Finally he said, "About this, yes."

"Fine! But I don't know how I'll get dressed if you're sleeping in the middle of *my* closet!"

"I'll put the mattress in the space between the bed and the wall. During the day, I'll slide it under your bed. No one will ever know it's there."

She blinked several times in surprise. It sounded as though he'd thought things out already. "I guess that would work. Are you sure you'll be comfortable?"

"I've slept on the floor more than once in my life. An air mattress will be a luxury. Is that it? Are we finished?"

Melissa stepped back as if he'd slapped her. "You don't have to show how eager you are to get away from me!" she snapped. "It doesn't bode well for the future."

He closed his eyes. "Lady, you have no idea. I'm trying to do what you want, but I can only handle so much."

Before she could even try to understand his words, he stalked out of the kitchen. She supposed he must be talking about his shoulder. She knew he was in pain, but she hadn't realized it was bothering him that much.

Terri came into the kitchen a few minutes later. "Has Dad gone? Did you ask him about me sleeping here?"

"Oh, honey, I'm sorry, I forgot," Melissa said. "It completely slipped my mind."

Terri grinned. "Yeah, I've heard love will do that to you."

Melissa gave her a weak smile. "Um, I think you should go back to your dad's house tonight. He'll need someone to rub liniment into his shoulder in the morning. It would be good if you're there to take care of it for him." She knew he wasn't going to ask for *her* help.

Disappointment filled Terri's face. "I guess you're right. But I brought a lot of my things over."

"I know. And I promise I'll ask him. But he'll need you in the morning."

"Okay. I'd better go before he goes to sleep. He's not easy to wake up, you know."

"He works hard."

"Yeah, he's a pretty good dad," Terri said, her smile indulgent.

Melissa hugged her. "Yes, he is. In fact, he may be the best dad in the world. Both of you can come up for breakfast in the morning. I don't think your dad is going to work in the morning."

"Really? Wow, he must be hurt worse than I

thought.'' Terri immediately started out of the kitchen.

Melissa would've reassured her, but the girl was too eager to check on her father. Calling good-night, Melissa let her go. She'd soon find out Rob was okay.

As okay as a miserable man could be.

Again she wondered if she should free him from his promise. But her original plan had bogged them down in a series of events that seemed impossible to break from. If they didn't marry, Mr. Graham would take Wayne, Billy and Susie and separate them.

But even if the children's future wasn't involved, Melissa felt a reluctance to sever her relationship with Rob. It alarmed her to realize how much her thoughts, her world, centered around the man. Her life would be empty without Rob and Terri. But most especially Rob.

With a sigh, she finally admitted to herself that she cared for him. That she wanted to care for him, make him smile, love him. When she slid a hot meal in front of him at the end of a long day and watched him appreciatively inhale its scent, joy filled her heart.

Today, when she'd rubbed the liniment into his shoulder, she'd delighted in doing more for him. And having the opportunity to touch him. He was fearlessly independent and tried to keep his distance, except for the few times he'd kissed her.

Obviously her kisses weren't as addictive for him as his were for her. If they were, he wouldn't hustle out of any room she occupied.

With an indulgent sniff, she tidied the kitchen,

then locked up and climbed the stairs. She checked on all the children. Wayne was the only one still awake, the light over his bed shining on the book he was reading. Billy, in the bed across from Wayne, was softly snoring.

"You'd better get to sleep, Wayne," Melissa suggested, a gentle smile on her face.

"Okay, as soon as I finish this chapter," he assured her. "Has Rob gone home?"

"Yes, he has."

"I'll be glad when you're married. Then he'll stay here, and we'll seem more like a family."

"Yes, that will be nice, won't it?" she agreed, then softly closed the door and turned to her own room.

Yes, it would be nice, but she'd still have to keep her distance, because that was the way Rob wanted it.

With a sigh, she sank down onto her bed. Then her chin lifted and she promised herself she'd just have to change his mind.

Rob had been ashamed of himself the night before. He'd forgotten all about Terri when he'd stormed out of Melissa's house, determined to keep his distance from the woman he wanted more than any woman in the world.

Until Terri had shown up at the house.

This morning, she knocked on his bedroom door. "Dad, are you in there?"

"Yeah," he replied, groaning. His shoulder was damned stiff and painful this morning.

Terri opened the door and stuck her head in. "I've

got the liniment here. Melissa said for me to rub it on your shoulder this morning. Okay?''

"That would be great, baby.''

He scooted over so Terri could sit on the edge of the bed. He wanted to keep his distance from Melissa, but he appreciated the care she showed him.

Terri began rubbing the shoulder. Gradually the pain and stiffness eased. ''That's great, Terri. Now, if you'll bring me some aspirin and a glass of water, I may feel half human again.''

"Dad!'' she said with a laugh. ''I'll be right back. You start getting dressed because Melissa is fixing breakfast.''

"No! We can eat breakfast here!''

"She offered last night and I agreed. I thought you'd want to see her first thing in the morning.'' Again she laughed.

"Uh, yeah. Okay. After breakfast, I have some errands to run.''

"Oh, I hope you don't need me to help you. Melissa and I are going to the mall again.''

"The mall?'' he asked, a sense of horror in his words.

"Quit teasing, Dad. We have to do things for the wedding. And we get to taste the wedding cakes!''

He didn't understand the fascination, but he nodded as if he did. ''Okay. Need some money?''

"Well, I'd like to buy a new dress for the wedding. Whatever Melissa wants me to wear.''

"Sure. I'll write Melissa a check and she can pay for your dress and…and whatever else you need.''

"Thanks, Dad. You're the best!''

Even as he made those arrangements, after a great

breakfast, Rob managed to keep his distance from Melissa. It wasn't too difficult with all the children awake and making demands. He wondered what real couples did to ensure their privacy when children were involved.

He invited Wayne to accompany him, as his best man, on his errands that morning. Then he caught a glimpse of Billy's disappointed face. "Maybe you should come with us, Billy, unless you don't want to. We could probably use a little help."

The boy beamed at him. "Okay! I don't know anything about marrying, though," he added, a worried look filling his eyes.

"Don't worry, son. You'll know enough," Rob assured him, avoiding Melissa's gaze.

He'd almost escaped with the boys, when Terri reminded him to kiss Melissa goodbye. The excitement that filled him at the excuse to hold her was disturbing. He shouldn't want this so much, he warned himself.

Then he pulled her against him, and his lips covered hers. He'd intended a brief, sexless touch. It turned into a sizzling, all-consuming kiss.

"Dad! You're getting carried away!" Terri called, laughing. "We want to get to the stores sometime today."

He pulled away from Melissa, still wrapped in her sensuality, his gaze focused on those soft lips. They were trembling, he realized. His gaze lifted to her eyes. Was she upset? Did she hate him to touch her?

She licked her lips, then said, "I guess we'd better go. Shopping. We...have a lot to do."

"Yeah," he agreed.

He had something to do, too. If he could only remember what it was.

July fourth dawned bright and early. Rob lay in his bed, thinking about the events that were to take place that day. He was ready. As ready as he'd ever be to commit to a woman he loved, who loved children instead of him.

He'd made a mistake in his first marriage, choosing a woman who loved herself more than anyone. Now he was marrying a woman who loved everyone else. Why couldn't he get it right?

With a grunt, he rolled out of bed. No reason to spend a lot of time moaning about his situation. He was committed to Melissa, and he wouldn't change that now, even if he could. As miserable as he was being with her but not able to touch her, he'd be more miserable without her.

Both he and Terri had fallen under Melissa's spell, just as her other children had. None of them wanted to be apart from her. Today would link them all together. As Wayne had once said, they would become a family.

A knock on his front door dragged him from the bed. Pulling on a pair of jeans, he buttoned them on the way to the door.

Wayne and Billy were standing on his porch, several dishes in their hands.

"Hey, guys, what's this?"

"Breakfast," Wayne announced, a grin on his face. "Melissa says you can't see her before the wedding, but she didn't want you to be hungry."

Rob smiled back. Did the woman think he was

helpless? He'd been getting his own breakfast for a few years now. But it wouldn't taste as good as Melissa's, he admitted.

"Come on in. I'm starving."

"We're eating with you," Billy informed him, "'cause we're guys. Melissa says only ladies in her house today."

"I'm grateful for the company." And he was. It took his mind off the wedding. Sort of.

Her wedding day.

Melissa was up early. No laying in bed for her. She had too much to do. By the time she sent the boys to Rob's with breakfast, she was far along on her list of things to do.

"Melissa?" Beth called from the front door.

When she reached the door to the kitchen, both Beth and Abby were in the house, heading toward her.

"Hi. I didn't know you were coming over."

"We thought maybe you'd still be in bed," Abby said with a grin. "We were going to fix you breakfast in bed."

Melissa rolled her eyes. "Today? I don't have time to laze around."

"It's your wedding day. You're supposed to take it easy," Beth assured her.

"I am. Did I tell you I've arranged for Jennifer, the lady from the Classic Cuts shop, to come out and do our hair and nails?" Melissa asked, leading the way back to the kitchen. There was still some coffee left in the pot.

"Who? You and Terri?" Beth asked. "I wonder

if she'd have time to do me, too. I haven't had a manicure since *I* got married."

"She might. And she's going to do the little girls, too. I thought they should have some of the fun."

"Is there anything we can do for you?" Abby asked. "Ellen is planning on coming over as soon as she finishes making mounds of potato salad."

Melissa sat down at the table, after pouring them all coffee, and indulged in her emotions. "Tell me I'm doing the right thing."

Both her sisters looked shocked. Abby leaned forward. "You were the one insisting on marrying so soon, Melissa. Have you changed your mind?"

"No, of course not," she immediately replied. "I'm just—it's a little scary. And frustrating. Rob doesn't—he's a good man."

"Yes, he is," Beth said. "Jed likes him."

Which of course, was the deciding factor in everything for Beth, Melissa realized with a smile. But it didn't do that much for her.

"Rob doesn't what?" Abby asked.

"He's not interested in me," Melissa finally said. "He's so good with the children. Wayne and Billy follow him around like puppies. And the little girls, they attack him every time he comes in, wanting hugs and kisses. He's made such a difference in Jessica and Mary Ann."

"How do you feel about hugs and kisses?" Abby asked softly, her gaze fixed on Melissa.

Trust Abby to zero in on the problem.

She seized her courage and faced Abby. "I want them, too. Sometimes I think he…he wants me. But other times, it seems he avoids me."

Beth hooted with laughter.

"What's so funny?" Melissa asked, hurt, her eyes filling with tears. How could her sister be so insensitive?

"It's a good thing I'm married," Beth said smugly.

Abby frowned at her. "I don't think your marriage has anything to do with—"

"Otherwise, we wouldn't know what's going on," Beth interrupted. She reached for Melissa's hand. "Jed said Rob is utterly miserable."

When Melissa would've left the room to go sob in private, Beth held her back.

"Melissa, he's miserable because he's completely in love with you."

Melissa stopped struggling and stared at her sister. "What did you say?"

"How do you know?" Abby asked.

"That's why I said it's a good thing I got married. I didn't know. But Jed said he felt sorry for Rob. When I asked why, he said Rob reminded him of himself before we worked out our difficulties."

Hope rose in Melissa. "Do you think it's true?"

Beth, of course, had absolute faith in Jed's opinion and immediately assured her sister of it. Abby wasn't quite as convinced. "She could be right. I've seen him watching you," she said.

"I've thought—when he kisses me—to convince the kids, you know, I've thought he enjoyed it." She hated the fact that her cheeks were turning red, but just thinking of those moments embarrassed her.

"Well, tonight, you should put on your sexiest nightgown and see what happens," Beth suggested.

Melissa turned an even brighter red.

"I don't think that's the way to go about it," Abby protested. "It shouldn't be an impulse. I mean, marriage is important. It should be a conscious decision."

"My way works faster," Beth argued.

Melissa put her hands to her head, unsure what to think. She wanted to believe Rob cared about her, wanted her. But maybe he didn't want her. Maybe he just wanted a mother for Terri. If that was all—

"Melissa, the lady's here to do our hair," Terri called from the entry.

"Looks like the time for talking is over," Abby said, "if you're going to go through with this wedding."

Melissa knew the response to that statement. She was going to be married today, no matter what.

She mulled over Beth's words while she got ready. She wanted to believe them. The more she thought, the more she decided Rob did want her. Men wanted sex—without the emotional trappings.

But she wanted more. She'd finally found a man who would accept her dream—a houseful of children. Rob was wonderful with the children.

Only she'd discovered that wasn't enough. She wanted a man who loved her even more than the children. Not wanted her. Loved her. Who would marry her because he wanted to spend his life with her. Not the children.

Rob might want sex. He might love the children.

But she wanted him to love her.

It seemed the entire community had arrived at the Circle K for the wedding, Rob decided as he stood in the shadow of the barn watching them mill about.

"How much longer?" Wayne asked, standing beside him.

"I reckon it's about time. Jim Bob and the other musicians are picking up their instruments," he assured the boy. He'd been given strict instructions by Ellen. He and Wayne were to go stand in front of the arbor of roses that had been placed in front of the big shade tree beside the main house, joining the minister. Rob could see him moving into place now.

"Come on, son," he said, putting a hand on Wayne's shoulder as the fiddler began a stylized version of "The Wedding March." "That's our cue."

A strange calm had descended over Rob as the time had drawn closer. He didn't know how he'd feel tomorrow, but today, he was doing the right thing. The good thing.

As he and Wayne took their places, everyone began to fill the folded chairs arranged in rows with an aisle down the center. The aisle Melissa would use to come to his side.

When the three little girls, stair step in size, came out of the main house, each carrying a basket of rose petals, he took a deep gulp of air. Yeah, the right thing.

They wore soft pink sundresses, with matching pink sandals, and they looked adorable. Mary Ann beamed at him as she led the way. It surprised him that they'd convinced her to do such a bold thing.

She never hesitated, however, coming to stand beside him and tug on his pressed jeans.

"Rob!" she whispered, when he didn't respond.

Bending down, he said, "Yes, Mary Ann?"

"I have a new dress."

There were a few chuckles from the folks closest to the altar. Rob ignored them and kissed the little girl's cheek. "I know, and you look beautiful."

Not wanting to play favorites, he kissed Susie and Jessica, also.

Then Billy came down the aisle, bearing a pillow with a gold band taped to it. Rob knew it wasn't the wedding ring he'd picked out for Melissa, but Billy had needed a reason to come down the aisle with a bunch of girls.

The boy moved over to stand beside Wayne.

Next came his own daughter. His little girl. Only she looked about sixteen in a pink sundress just a little darker than the others. Her hair was all dark curls and pink flowers, making her look beautiful.

He heard Wayne clear his throat and glanced at the boy to see his gaze fixed on Terri. Man, he was going to have to keep his eye on those two. One more thing to worry about.

Then he stopped worrying.

He stopped thinking.

He stared.

A simple wedding. That's what Melissa had said. They'd be casual. He'd thought she wouldn't look like a bride.

He'd been wrong.

She was wearing a white silk blouse, trimmed in lace, its scooped neckline hinting at her charms. Tiny capped sleeves ended in lace. A flowing, filmy white skirt, tight around her small waist, swirled around her, making her look as if she were floating.

In her dark hair she wore a circlet of fresh flowers with a fingertip veil attached. Her bouquet wasn't the traditional white orchids. It was a vibrant mixture of color, a celebration of life. Suddenly he was glad Melissa had arranged for a photographer.

He wanted a picture of his bride so he'd never forget her breathtaking beauty.

He wanted to remember this day, in all its glory, no matter what came next. He figured he was as close to heaven as he'd ever come.

He was marrying Melissa.

Chapter Twelve

"**Y**ou may kiss your bride," the minister said.

Melissa faced her husband, her fingers trembling in his hands. He let them go and lifted her short veil, his gaze fixed on hers.

Was he asking permission? she wondered. Didn't he know she longed for his kisses? She'd never shoved him away, never been the one to end their rare embraces. Was he going to embarrass her in front of the entire community by *not* kissing her?

He answered that question by covering her mouth with his, his lips caressing hers as he pulled her body against his hard muscles.

"Ahem," the minister said, breaking them apart. He beamed at both of them, as if they'd passed some test. Then he turned them to face the crowd. "Ladies and gentlemen, may I present Mr. and Mrs. Rob Hanson."

The burst of applause startled Melissa. She was

wrapped in a sensual haze from the kiss Rob had given her, his strong arm around her waist. He led her up the aisle as their guests stood, still clapping.

When they reached the end of the aisle, Rob leaned over and whispered, "What do we do now?"

"We're going to go to the dance platform the cowboys built yesterday. We'll have our first dance. Then, in a little while, we'll have the barbecue dinner." She took a deep breath. "Then we'll cut the wedding cake."

That brief summary of their plans was all the talking they could do before they were surrounded by well-wishers. Melissa received a lot of kisses on her cheeks, while Rob's hand was pumped by the men. A few of the women gave him some kisses, too.

Then Rob led her to the dance floor, sheets of plyboard nailed onto a frame a foot up from the ground. The musicians began a waltz, and Rob gathered her to him again.

She sighed, feeling she'd come home, as she rested against him. His lips pressed against her hair as he moved her around the floor. She was scarcely aware of their audience. Her world began and ended with Rob.

Halfway through the dance, a burst of applause alerted them to a change. Melissa looked over Rob's shoulder and saw Wayne lead Terri to the middle of the floor. Their style of dance was a little different, with a lot more distance between their bodies, but it was sweet.

Then Billy and the three little girls formed a circle, amid laughter, and did their own style of dancing. Melissa looked up to see Rob's warm gaze, a gentleness on his lips that thrilled her. Then he waved a hand at their audience. "Join us," he called.

Soon a number of their neighbors were spinning to the music. Rob led Melissa to the side as the pace of the music changed. "I'm not too good with this fast stuff."

"That's okay. I'm not either," She wanted to be held in her husband's arms, not jump around on her own. "Are you hungry?"

His head whipped around from watching the dancers to stare at her, and Melissa wondered what about her words had bothered him. She hurriedly added, "Ellen and some friends are uncovering the food now."

"Oh. Food. Yeah. That would be good."

Her cheeks flushed as she wondered.... Fortunately, Ellen tapped her on the shoulder.

"Melissa, we're ready to start serving. You two should lead the way."

"Thank you, Ellen. Where are the children? I want them to go with us."

The dancing and eating continued for several more hours. As dusk began to fall, however, a quietness settled over the crowd. Then the fireworks began.

For half an hour, the sky, as it slowly darkened, was filled with sparkling lights, showers of stars that burned out, only to be replaced by more.

Precautions had been taken to ensure there were no brush fires. Some cowboys were spread out over the area, with water and feed sacks to beat out any sparks that might survive.

It was a glorious end to an incredible day, Melissa thought as she leaned against Rob, watching the fireworks. Her wedding was all she'd dreamed of, wished for. A gathering of people she loved, a celebration of togetherness, the start of a new life. She ignored the fact that she didn't believe her husband loved her.

She wasn't going to spoil her perfect day.

Rob didn't want the day to end. As long as they were among their neighbors, he could pretend. Pretend his bride loved him, as he loved her. Pretend their future was as bright as the fireworks. Pretend it would last forever.

He could hold her against him, drop kisses on her unsuspecting lips. He never had to leave her side. He didn't have to pretend an indifference that was killing him.

As they sat there, a couple, they were surrounded by the six children. Mary Ann crawled up into Rob's lap as the hour grew late. Then he added Jessica, and Melissa held Susie.

Wayne and Billy sat on the grass beside their chairs. Terri joined them, but only after she spread out a cup towel to avoid grass stains on her dress.

Together they watched the fireworks, said goodbye to their guests and visited with Abby, Beth, Jed, Ellen and the cowboys as the day ended.

They were a family.

Abby had offered for all the children to spend the night at the main house. After all, it was their wedding night, she'd pointed out.

With her cheeks fiery red, Melissa had quickly refused. That was all she needed, to be alone with Rob when nothing was going to happen.

She wanted something to happen. But sex wasn't the important thing. She wanted Rob to tell her he loved her. *Then* she wanted him to show her with every muscle he owned. Until he did that, there'd be no real wedding night.

Rob helped her tuck the children into bed. Even the two older ones, Terri and Wayne, were exhausted. Quickly the house settled into its late-night sounds.

Children sleeping.

Awkwardly, she and Rob stared at each other.

"Uh, do you want anything to eat?" she asked.

"No. The barbecue was great."

"Yes." The only sound was the grandfather clock in the hallway ticking off the seconds. "Well, um, I guess I'll go to bed."

"I'll be up later. Uh, where is the mattress? I don't want to wake you when I come to…when I go to sleep."

"It's already blown up. I slid it under my bed, like you said. And it has sheets and a blanket on it. You can take the other pillow from my bed."

"Okay, thanks."

She stood there, staring at him, wishing things were different, hoping—abruptly she turned and fled up the stairs.

Rob watched her go, his body aching with desire. His wife. He loved her. But all she wanted was a father for the children.

With a weary sigh, he turned to the kitchen. Not for food. But he could make a cup of coffee. That would give him something to do. Because he didn't dare go to bed until Melissa was already asleep.

Two hours later, when he finally got the nerve to open the bedroom door, the moonlight from the window beside the bed showed Melissa curled into a tight ball in the center of the big bed.

Rob, carrying his boots in his hand, tiptoed past the bed, keeping his gaze averted from her sleeping form. He undressed in the bath, neatly folding his clothes. Then he reentered the bedroom. With a sigh, he indulged himself by staring at her. Damn, he wanted her. He wanted to hold her, love her, know that he could wake up beside her.

With a swiftly swallowed laugh that had more than a touch of bitterness, he reminded himself that he would wake up beside her. Only not in the bed.

He pulled the mattress out from under the bed, gently removed the pillow from Melissa's bed, and sank down onto his makeshift bed. Stretching out with a sigh, he tried to shut out Melissa's breathing as he closed his eyes.

It was going to be a long night.

Rob pulled his horse to a halt at the crest of the hill and watched the scene below him. He and Wayne were helping work the cattle today because he felt guilty. They'd only started ProRide a few weeks ago, and already it was consuming his time.

In fact, he'd talked to Abby about hiring another foreman for the cattle operations. With Jed's connections, their rodeo horse company was taking off faster than any of them had expected.

"Everything okay?" Wayne asked, pulling his mount up beside Rob's.

"Fine. You okay? It's been a hard day."

Wayne grinned back, the look of a boy doing exactly what he loved. "Hell—I mean, heck, just call me Brier Rabbit," he returned, mentioning the sneaky rabbit who had pleaded not to be given what he loved. Then he urged his horse down the hill to catch up with the herd of cows.

Rob smiled. Wayne was a good kid. And a hard worker. Billy, this morning, had asked when he would be allowed to ride out with them. Rob supposed he'd need to start bringing the boy out for half days.

He'd discovered he liked working with the kids. The little girls reminded him of Terri's younger years. They always smelled sweet and were warm and cuddly. Terri was happy, too. She'd gone with him and Wayne on trips to look at horses, but she loved being at home with Melissa.

So did he.

In spite of the fight to keep his desires under control, Rob loved every minute spent next to his wife. He treasured those words, murmuring them to himself. *His wife.*

Life had actually been easier, in spite of his fears. He didn't get as much sleep, of course. Lying on the air mattress beside her bed, he never slept until after her quiet, even breathing told him she'd drifted off.

Then he'd rise and watch her sleep, enjoy her defenseless ease, her total relaxation. When she was awake, she seemed tense around him. Once or twice, he'd even leaned close as she slept to touch her soft

hair, to smell the sweet scent of her. But he didn't
do that often. He was afraid she'd awaken and be
frightened.

He stayed in a perpetual state of arousal, but the
pain was worth being near her. He loved her. More
than he'd ever thought possible. If he was never to
have a true marriage, if he was never to be able to
touch her, he wouldn't trade what he had. At least
he got to be with her.

With a sigh, he set his horse toward the herd, to
catch up with the others.

"Did everyone make their bed?" Melissa asked
the children as they gathered at the table for their
midmorning snack.

Even Mary Ann nodded her head.

Billy, in typical male fashion, said, "I don't see
why we have to make our beds. We just get back in
them again tonight."

"We make our beds," Melissa told him, "because
we want to have warm cookies as they come out of
the oven."

"All right!" he agreed with enthusiasm.

She laughed, enjoying the normalcy of the moment. The Prine children, while still missing their
parents, were dealing with their sorrow. They were
growing and learning and living. Mary Ann and Jessica didn't miss their parents. But they were happy.

She and Terri had become so close, they could
almost read each other's mind. Which was a fright-
ening thought when she thought about Terri's father.
Which she did frequently, with a longing so intense
she did her best to hide it.

"You made cookies?" Terri asked. "I thought you were cleaning upstairs."

"I decided cookies were more important. Besides, the lady I hired to clean is coming this morning for the first time. I wanted to leave her something to do." She grinned at the teenager and found an answering response.

Life was good.

A knock on the door interrupted them. "That will be Mrs. Brown," Melissa said. "Terri, would you show her in?"

The woman lived down the road. All her children were in school and she'd agreed to come at ten three days a week to work for five hours.

Terri hurried out of the kitchen. When she reappeared at the door of the kitchen a couple of minutes later, Melissa knew something was wrong. Terri looked frightened.

"What is it?" she asked hurriedly, instinctively moving toward the girl.

"It's Mr. Graham."

Melissa frowned. The man hadn't visited since their wedding several weeks ago. Nothing could be wrong. She and Rob had been very careful about the exact nature of their marriage. There'd been no rumors.

"Is he in the living room? I'll go speak to him. You take the cookies out of the oven. As soon as they've cooled a little, the children may each have two, with a glass of milk."

She left the kitchen, pasting a polite smile on her face. When she entered the seldom-used living room, she discovered Mr. Graham was not alone.

"Mrs. Hanson, let me introduce Mr. and Mrs. Bodine."

Melissa greeted them, her mind trying to figure out why they were there. Mr. Graham explained at once.

"The Bodines are interested in adopting Susie."

"No!" The word burst out of her before she could stop it. "You don't mean it."

"Why not?" the woman asked, stepping forward. "Is there something wrong with her?"

In spite of the urge to lie, Melissa couldn't. "No, there's nothing wrong with her. But…her brothers. Are you interested in adopting her brothers?" She *might* be able to let the children go if they went together. Maybe.

The man put an arm around his wife. "No, we're not. I'm sure Mr. Graham will find someone else to take them. But my wife is delicate. She couldn't handle three children. We actually wanted a baby, but there aren't any available."

"Mr. Graham, you can't—"

"Mrs. Hanson, the children are wards of the state. It's my duty to find permanent homes for them," he said sternly. "Please bring Susie in here."

Melissa bit down on her bottom lip so hard she thought she tasted blood. Or maybe that was fear. "Perhaps you should join us in the kitchen. The children are having a midmorning snack. I'll pour you some coffee."

Without waiting for an answer, she led the way into the big, homey kitchen.

Once everyone was seated, the children unconcerned about the new arrivals, the woman asked Melissa several pointed questions about Susie. Melissa caught Billy's sudden alarm and smiled reassuringly.

This couldn't be happening. They couldn't take one of her children. She'd find a way, somehow.

Then the woman asked about Mary Ann. "She's cute and she's younger. Is it possible to—"

"No. Because we haven't found the parents, she's unavailable," Mr. Graham explained.

Melissa suddenly prayed they never found those miserable parents.

After a few tense moments Mr. Graham and the Bodines rose and Melissa escorted them to the door.

"Shall we make arrangements to take Susie out for a visit?" Mr. Graham suggested, smiling encouragingly at the couple.

"Yes, of course. Since we can't have a baby, I suppose she will do," the woman said, and her words made Melissa sick to her stomach. Susie "would do"?

Mr. Graham suggested Thursday, two days away, and a time, and all Melissa could do was nod. When the three had left, she didn't return to the kitchen. Instead she paced the entryway, trying to figure out how to stop the adoption.

Because she feared the people would take Susie away. She wasn't what they wanted, but they'd take her. They'd break up a family. And those people wouldn't love Susie as they all loved her.

Jessica and Mary Ann thought of her as their sister. So did Terri. Wayne and Billy adored their little sister. Rob—Rob would help her think of something. With a sense of relief, she ran for the phone in the den. Rob carried a cellular phone with him.

She wasn't alone. She had a husband, a husband she loved, who would help her save their family.

"Rob?" Relief flooded her as he answered the phone. "Rob, Mr. Graham came today. He brought a couple who want to adopt Susie."

"Melissa, slow down. Say that again?" he asked in comforting, solid tones.

She repeated her words, her heart breaking as the reality of the situation struck her. Tears filled her eyes. "Oh, Rob, we can't let them. They don't want the boys, just Susie. It will break all their hearts."

She looked up at that moment to see a stricken Billy staring at her. "Billy! Wait. Rob's going to—"

She never got to finish her sentence. The boy ran up the stairs.

"Billy heard me," she explained.

"Wayne and I will be there in a few minutes. Hang on, sweetheart. We'll figure something out."

Melissa hung up the phone with hope for the first time since Mr. Graham had announced the reason for his visit. Rob might not love her, as she wanted him to, he might not hold her through the night, but he was her husband. He would help her fight for their family.

She hurried up the stairs after Billy.

Rob caught up with Abby.

"I've got a little problem back at the house. Wayne and I need to go. Can you manage?"

"Sure. Is everything all right?"

"Graham wants to let a couple adopt Susie," Rob said succinctly, knowing he wouldn't have to explain the havoc the man had created.

"Is there anything I can do?"

Rob shook his head.

He called Wayne and explained the problem as they rode back to the barn. Then he had to soothe Wayne's anger and assure him they'd find a way to avoid the adoption.

When they reached the barn, he left his horse with Wayne to be cared for. He'd already made up his mind what he should do. "After you take care of the horses, go to the house and tell Melissa I'm visiting with Mr. Graham. Then reassure your brother and sister, okay?"

"I should go with you!" Wayne protested.

Rob put a hand on the boy's shoulder. "I know you want to go, Wayne, but we each have a job to do here. You do yours and I'll do mine."

He hurried to his pickup and almost flooded the vehicle in his eagerness to reach town. When he arrived, Mr. Graham was in his office. Rob didn't wait to be announced.

"Mr. Graham, I'm Rob Hanson."

"Of course, Mr. Hanson. I remember you from the wedding. What can I do for you?"

Rob didn't waste any time. "You can tell those people Susie's not up for adoption."

Mr. Graham studied him and Rob stood still, his jaw firm, waiting.

"I can't do that. As wards of the state, the children need to be placed in a permanent home."

"Not if they have to be split up. You can't do that to those kids."

"There aren't too many couples willing to take on three children at once, especially as old as they are.

We have to do the best we can," the man said with a genial smile.

Rob leaned forward, placing both hands on the man's desk, and quietly said, "She's not going to leave her brothers."

"Now, Mr. Hanson, you can't—"

"Yes, I can. My wife and I will adopt them."

Mr. Graham seemed surprised. He frowned. "I'm not sure—"

"I am. Give me the papers to fill out."

"Mr. Hanson, you're only recently married."

"So?"

"Well, you and your wife haven't even had time to figure out if you'll stay together, much less—"

Pain sliced through Rob at the thought of leaving Melissa. No matter what their circumstances, he knew he'd never leave her.

"Mr. Graham. I love my wife more than life itself. We'll stay together."

"But, Mr. Hanson, adopting three children means you'll always have them. It's not something you do on a whim."

Rob straightened and chuckled. "Man, you don't have any idea what kind of woman Melissa is, do you?" When Mr. Graham stared at him, he continued, "She's a forever kind of woman. She loves those kids, and she's never going to let them go. Her heart is as big as the outdoors and just as true. It's no whim. Now, where are those papers?"

"This is highly irregular," the man grumbled, but since he was digging through a drawer to find the papers, Rob crossed his arms over his chest and remained silent.

He had no hesitation in saying he and Melissa would adopt the children, even though he hadn't discussed it with Melissa. He knew his wife. She was steadfast and true, and it filled him with love just to admit that. She wasn't like his first wife. She wouldn't abandon any child.

Or her husband.

They were going to have to have a talk. Their marriage was forever, too, and they should make it a real one. Even if she didn't love him, she'd married him. He wanted babies to add to their family. He wanted Melissa.

It was time he told her.

Melissa leaned against the wall outside Mr. Graham's office, tears running down her cheeks.

He loved her?

He'd said he did, but had he said it for Mr. Graham's benefit? Or did he mean it?

He was offering to adopt Wayne, Billy and Susie. Even if he didn't love her, she couldn't ask for more than that. But she was going to.

She wanted a real marriage. She wanted the right to hold Rob close, for him to hold her. She wanted a lifetime with him, with the children, with—

The sound of footsteps alerted her the interview was over. Rob opened the door, then came to an abrupt halt.

"Melissa! Are you all right?" he asked, reaching out for her.

She flew into his arms, loving the strength of him, the knowledge that he'd fought her battle for her. "I'm fine, now. Did you get the papers?"

"You heard? It's okay with you?"

Mr. Graham, on his heels, asked, outraged, "You mean you hadn't even discussed the adoption with your wife?"

Melissa raised her head, her mien proud. "He didn't have to, Mr. Graham. My husband knows me. He knows what I want." Her gaze settled on Rob's face and she fought the urge to spread kisses all over that firm jaw, those delicious lips.

Rob squeezed her waist, then moved her forward. "We need to get out of Mr. Graham's office, sweetheart. We'll have the papers back tomorrow," he assured the man, before guiding Melissa through the outside office to the sunshine.

"What are you doing here?" he asked once they were alone.

"Wayne told me where you were. I thought I should face Mr. Graham with you. I wanted to suggest we adopt the kids, but—"

"Then you agree?"

"Oh, yes."

"Okay. I'll follow you to the ranch."

He tried to walk her over to her car, but Melissa dug her heels into the grass. "No."

"No, what? How else—"

"I want to ride with you. We'll get my car later. We have some talking to do."

"I thought you wanted to adopt the kids?"

Melissa was tired of talking. Instead of answering, she slid her arms around his neck and kissed him.

Rob froze momentarily. Then his arms encircled her, squeezing her tightly against him, his lips taking over the kiss.

* * *

Mercy, he hadn't kissed Melissa like that since their wedding day. He couldn't. He might lose control. Then he remembered why he couldn't lose control right then. They were in the middle of town.

He didn't know what was going on, but he had to find out. If she was thanking him for his suggestion that they adopt, he was going to have to explain how dangerous her thank-you was.

"Come on." This time he didn't lead her to her car, but pulled her along to his truck. After helping her inside, he hurried to the driver's side. He got in and she slid across the bench seat to press against his side.

He stared at her. "Melissa, I know you're happy about the adoption, but...but you're asking for trouble."

She gave him a serene smile. "Just drive, Rob."

He frowned but did as she asked. It was hard to concentrate with her sweet body rubbing against his, fulfilling all his fantasies. He might have to go out and work half the night before he could sleep, to rid himself of the hot liquid of desire that was shooting through him.

He said nothing to Melissa. It was hard enough to concentrate on his driving.

"Turn here," she ordered a couple of miles out of town.

He automatically did as she asked. "Why? This leads to that little lake, but no place else. Where are we going?"

"Did I ever show you the favorite parking spot for the teenagers around here?"

That strange question brought his gaze to her face. "You're taking me parking?"

"Oh, yes," she assured him with enthusiasm that had his control nearly slipping.

"Stop here."

They were near the edge of the lake, sheltered beneath several trees. "Melissa—"

"Did you mean it?"

"I told you I did. I've got the papers right here."

"Did you mean it when you said you loved me?"

Rob caught his breath. He hadn't realized she'd heard those words. But if things were going to change, he knew he had to be honest now. "Yeah, I meant it."

He'd been staring straight ahead, but now her warm fingers took his chin and pulled him around to face her. "Then why haven't you said anything?"

"You told me you didn't want a real marriage."

"That's because you said you didn't!" she retorted, exasperation on her face.

"What was I supposed to say? That you were driving me crazy with your sexy body, your sweet smile, those tempting lips? We'd only known each other a couple of weeks. And my first marriage was...a disaster."

"Our marriage won't be a disaster," she assured him. Then she lifted her lips to his.

Rob pulled her even tighter against him. His lips urged hers to open to him and they melded together, finally free to show their love to each other.

Several minutes later, stretched out on the pickup bench seat, Rob lifted his lips from Melissa's.

"Damn. I dreamed of making love to you, but not in my pickup like a couple of randy teenagers!"

Melissa's cheeks pinkened. "We could wait until tonight, when the kids are in bed."

"Waiting isn't an option, but I have an idea."

He sat up and reached for his cell phone. His gaze remained on Melissa, who was rebuttoning her blouse. He wanted to tell her to stop, but he supposed she'd feel awkward driving down the road half naked. But he loved looking at her.

"Ellen? I have a big favor to ask. Could you take the children until bedtime this evening? I know it's a lot to ask, but Melissa and I need some time alone."

"Yeah," he agreed with a laugh, staring at his wife.

Melissa was grinning but her cheeks got even redder.

"Yeah, we'll owe you a big one. Thanks."

Then he dialed another number. "Wayne? Everything's all right. Susie's not going anywhere. We'll explain everything tonight. Right now, I want all of you to go over to Ellen's. She's going to feed you lunch and dinner."

He listened to Wayne's questions, then said, "I'll explain everything later. Right now, we need some time alone. You know how it is with newlyweds," he added.

Wayne's sudden silence told him the boy understood even as it embarrassed him. Then his quick agreement ended the conversation.

"Okay, Mrs. Hanson, we're going to start our very brief honeymoon in our very own bed. You notice I said our bed, because I'm through sleeping on that torturous air mattress.''

"Wasn't it comfortable?" Melissa asked, a frown on her face.

He leaned over and kissed her again, almost forgetting their plans. Finally pulling back, his breathing heavy, he said, "With you sleeping two feet away? No, sweetheart, it wasn't comfortable."

She snuggled up against him. "Then I'm glad you're going to be joining me in that big bed, because it wasn't very comfortable for me without you in it."

He pressed down on the gas and rushed toward home.

"I'm glad our first time will be at home, in our bed," Melissa added dreamily. "I'd hate to tell our children that we made love for the first time in your pickup truck at the lake."

"Not many people have to worry about explaining that to their kids when they marry," Rob said dryly.

"I know, but we're lucky."

He pulled her even more tightly against him, steering with one hand. "You're right, sweetheart. We are the luckiest people in the world."

And coming next month, older sister Abby meets her match in her new foreman, Logan Crawford. Look for CHERISH THE BOSS, *only from Silhouette Romance.*

Look Who's Celebrating Our 20th Anniversary:

"Happy 20th birthday, Silhouette. You made the writing dream of hundreds of women a reality. You enabled us to give [women] the stories [they] wanted to read and helped us teach [them] about the power of love."

—*New York Times* bestselling author
Debbie Macomber

"I wish you continued success, Silhouette Books.... Thank you for giving me a chance to do what I love best in all the world."

—International bestselling author
Diana Palmer

"A visit to Silhouette is a guaranteed happy ending, a chance to touch magic for a little while.... It refreshes and revitalizes and makes us feel better.... I hope Silhouette goes on forever."

—Award-winning bestselling author
Marie Ferrarella

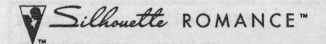

Silhouette ROMANCE™

Intimate Moments is celebrating Silhouette's 20ᵗʰ Anniversary with groundbreaking new promotions and star authors:

Look for these original novels from
New York Times bestselling authors:

In August 2000:
A Game of Chance by **Linda Howard**, #1021

In September 2000:
Night Shield by **Nora Roberts**,
part of NIGHT TALES

Don't miss
A YEAR OF LOVING DANGEROUSLY,
a twelve-book continuity series featuring SPEAR—a
covert intelligence agency. For its equally enigmatic
operatives, love was never part of the mission profile....
Sharon Sala launches the promotion in July 2000
with *Mission: Irresistible*, #1016.

In September 2000, look for the return
of **36 HOURS**, with original stories from
**Susan Mallery, Margaret Watson,
Doreen Roberts and Marilyn Pappano**.

And look for:
Who Do You Love?
October 2000, #1033
You won't want to miss this two-in-one collection
featuring **Maggie Shayne** and **Marilyn Pappano**!

Available at your favorite retail outlet.

Where love comes alive™

ATTENTION,
LINDSAY McKENNA FANS!

**Morgan Trayhern has three brand-new missions
in Lindsay McKenna's latest series:**

**Morgan's men are made for battle—
but are they ready for love?**

The excitement begins in July 2000, with
Lindsay McKenna's 50th book!

MAN OF PASSION

(Silhouette Special Edition® #1334)

Featuring rugged Rafe Antonio, aristocrat by birth,
loner by choice. But not for long....

Coming in November 2000:

A MAN ALONE

(Silhouette Special Edition® #1357)

Featuring Thane Hamilton, a wounded war hero on his way
home to the woman who has always secretly loved him....

*Look for the third book in the series in early 2001! In the
meantime, don't miss Lindsay McKenna's brand-new,
longer-length single title, available in August 2000:*

**MORGAN'S MERCENARIES:
HEART OF THE WARRIOR**

Only from Lindsay McKenna and
Silhouette Books!

COMING NEXT MONTH

#1462 THOSE MATCHMAKING BABIES—Marie Ferrarella
Storkville, USA
With the opening of her new day-care center, Hannah Brady was swamped. Then twin babies appeared at the back door! Luckily Dr. Jackson Caldwell was *very* willing to help. In fact, Hannah soon wondered if his interest wasn't more than neighborly....

#1463 CHERISH THE BOSS—Judy Christenberry
The Circle K Sisters
Abby Kennedy was not what Logan Crawford had expected in his new boss. The Circle K's feisty owner was young, intelligent...and beautiful. And though Abby knew a lot about ranching, Logan was hoping *he* could teach *her* a few things—about love!

#1464 FIRST TIME, FOREVER—Cara Colter
Virgin Brides
She was caring for her orphaned nephew. He had a farm to run and a toddler to raise. So Kathleen Miles and Evan Atkins decided on a practical, mutually beneficial union...until the handsome groom decided to claim his virgin bride....

#1465 THE PRINCE'S BRIDE-TO-BE—Valerie Parv
The Carramer Crown
As a favor to her twin sister, Caroline Temple agreed to pose as handsome Prince Michel de Marigny's betrothed. But soon she wanted to be the prince's real-life bride. Yet if he knew the truth, would Michel accept *Caroline* as his wife?

#1466 IN WANT OF A WIFE—Arlene James
Millionaire Channing Hawkins didn't want romance, but he needed a mommy for his daughter. Lovely Jolie Winters was a perfect maternal fit, but Channing soon realized he'd gotten more than he'd wished for...and that love might be part of the package....

#1467 HIS, HERS...OURS?—Natalie Patrick
Her boss was getting married, and perfectionist Shelley Harriman wanted everything flawless. But Wayne Perry, her boss's friend, had entirely different ideas. Could these two get through planning the wedding...and admit there might be another in *their* future?

CMN0700